"Schogt is a consumm
A gripping fictional tale of i
An intrepid and remar
—Hans Christian von Baeyer,
author of *Taming the Atom*

"A delight . . . Provides excellent and entertaining insights
into the lives and ill-understood drives
of working mathematicians. I strongly recommend it."
—Sir Roger Penrose,
author of *The Emperor's New Mind*

"Lighthearted, enjoyable."
—*Library Journal*

"In a denouement that reveals more about the nature
of human desires than about wild numbers,
Schogt deftly reveals how intellectual ambition actually
feeds—and is fed by—love . . . Impressive."
—*ALA Booklist*

PHILIBERT SCHOGT holds a degree in philosophy and mathematics.
The Wild Numbers is his first novel. He lives in Amsterdam.

The Wild Numbers

Philibert Schogt

A PLUME BOOK

PLUME
Published by the Penguin Group
Penguin Putnam Inc., 375 Hudson Street, New York, New York 10014, U.S.A.
Penguin Books Ltd, 27 Wrights Lane, London W8 5TZ, England
Penguin Books Australia Ltd, Ringwood, Victoria, Australia
Penguin Books Canada Ltd, 10 Alcorn Avenue, Toronto, Ontario, Canada M4V 3B2
Penguin Books (N.Z.) Ltd, 182–190 Wairau Road, Auckland 10, New Zealand

Penguin Books Ltd, Registered Offices: Harmondsworth, Middlesex, England

Published by Plume, a member of Penguin Putnam Inc. This is an authorized reprint of a hardcover edition published by Four Walls Eight Windows. For information address Four Walls Eight Windows, 39 West 14th Street, Room 503, New York, New York, 10011.

Four Walls Eight Windows Printing, April 2000
First Plume Printing, May 2001
10 9 8 7 6 5 4 3 2 1

First published in 1999 as *De wilde getallen* (Uitgeverij De Arbeiderspers, Amsterdam).

The Library of Congress has catalogued the Four Walls Eight Windows edition as follows:

Schogt, Philibert.
[Wilde getallen. English] The Wild Numbers / Philibert Schogt.
p. cm.
ISBN 1-56858-166-1 (hc.)
0-452-28247-0 (pbk.)
PT5881.29C4964 W5513 2000
839.3'1364—dc21 99-086581

Printed in the United States of America
Original hardcover design by Ink, Inc.

The Wild Numbers

1

Five plus three equals eight. It always has and it always will, of course, but it had never felt as exhilarating as it did this Thursday morning. I had just woken up and was doing my arithmetic, a daily exercise that helps clear the fog left by my dreams. Two plus five, twelve minus eight, sometimes I might throw in a seventeen times forty-one. Nothing too strenuous, though: the silliest injury that an athlete can suffer is to pull a muscle during warm-up. Normally I have to keep going for quite a while before gathering the courage to get out of bed, but today, adding three to five was more than enough. Life was beautiful and this was going to be my day.

After a quick breakfast on my balcony, I took the elevator down to the basement to get my bicycle. Although it is downhill all the way to the campus, I took my time today. Like a young father with a new sense of responsibility, I have become extremely cautious in traffic since my recent discovery. Besides, it was already quite hot and muggy, and I didn't want to sweat too much on my way to an important meeting.

Now that the exams had been written and marked, the campus was almost deserted. On the central field, sputtering jets of water from numerous sprinklers swept across the yellowing grass. I locked my bicycle by the east wing of the Math and Computer Science Building but should have known better; the doors were tightly bolted, so that I had to walk around to the main entrance.

I stopped in my office to pick up a copy of my manuscript, then continued down the long corridor. Most of my colleagues were already on vacation, but Larry Oberdorfer's door was open. He was working on his computer, smiling to himself as always.

"Well well well," he called out to me. "We've been seeing an awful lot of you lately!"

"I've come to see Dimitri," I said, and left it at that.

Well well well, in other words: what was a mediocre mathematician like me doing down at the office in his free time? If only he knew!

As I approached Dimitri's office, I could not help becoming nervous. Dimitri Arkanov is the Grand Old Man of our faculty. Five years ago he reached retirement age and was taken off the payroll, but he has stayed on as an emeritus professor and is still the first to arrive every morning, his mind as powerful and agile as ever.

When I entered his room, he was standing by the window looking out over the campus grounds, absorbed in thoughts quite probably beyond my capacity to understand.

"Sit down, Isaac," he said without turning around, "Sit down."

My stomach muscles contracted when I saw my article lying on his desk, bloodied with illegible comments in red ink. I told myself that there was little cause for concern: I had sat here last week while Dimitri paced up and down the room interrogating me about every step of my proof and turning the argument inside out to find possible errors. The sun had already set when he had finally poured out two generous glasses of cognac to toast the birth of a new theorem. He did insist that I show him the final draft of my article before sending it off to *Number*, not because he suspected we had overlooked something, but to make sure I had worked out my proof in sufficient detail for it to be understandable, if not to the general public, at least to the average reader of

Number. I still had trouble believing my good fortune, however. Although it was highly improbable, it could not be ruled out that he had spotted a fatal flaw after all. The red ink worried me.

"Too many sprinklers," he muttered. He sat down across from me and let his hand rest on my manuscript as if it were the Bible. "Isaac," he said with a solemn voice, "It was as great a joy reading this as it was the first time. Maybe even greater, for now I had the leisure to consider the far-reaching consequences of your theorem. Exactly as I had hoped when researching this problem more than thirty years ago, your findings lead directly into the high country of number theory. The view you offer is breathtaking."

I acknowledged the compliment with a slight nod, though inwardly I glowed with pride.

"Let me show you something." Dimitri tore a leaf from a note book and scribbled down a series of spectacular equations linking hitherto unrelated concepts, explaining how they followed more or less directly from my theorem. He soon reached the bottom of the page and tore out a second leaf.

I didn't quite understand what he was driving at; to be honest, I didn't understand at all (in mathematics, either you get it or you don't), but I was too happy to mind. It was hard to believe that only ten days ago, I was such a wreck that Dimitri had suggested I go on leave, well-meant advice that had further demoralized me. Now, we were walking through the high country together. I could have spent hours just listening to the great Dimitri Arkanov "sharing" his thoughts with me–and probably would have, if it had not been for someone knocking on the door. Dimitri was too absorbed in his mathematical explorations to notice, forcing me to interrupt his enthusiastic monologue.

"I see," he said, studying the door with a frown. There was another knock. "Yes?"

It was Mr. Vale. In spite of the heat wave, he was wearing his tweed suit. "Good morning, Professor Arkanov," he said with a deep bow. "Good morning, Professor Swift. What a stroke of luck to encounter you here. It was you I was looking for."

This past week, he had not so much as crossed my mind. As if to make up for this unusual and blissful absence from my thoughts, he had chosen the worst possible moment to reappear. I had a strong urge to push him back into the hall.

Dimitri, however, was amicable as always. "And a good morning to you, Mr. Vale!" he cried. "What a surprise to see you here on a Thursday."

"I'm dreadfully sorry to disturb you with this inopportune visit," Mr. Vale said, "the sole purpose of which is to remind Professor Swift of our appointment tomorrow afternoon."

"That's quite all right," I said, smiling pleasantly. Sure enough, I had forgotten all about our appointment.

"It so happened that I was in the neighborhood, and as I wasn't sure whether your distinguished colleague Professor Lasalle had asked you to attend the presentation of my newest research results in her stead–it may have slipped her mind, what with all the exams she had to mark and the excitement of her daughter's upcoming performance as Titania in *A Midsummer Night's Dream*..."

As his tiresome speech continued, he kept coming closer to the desk. I managed to cover up my own copy of my article with a sheet of paper, but when I reached over the desk intending to conceal Dimitri's copy as well, I sensed that I was being too obvious and quickly withdrew my hand. The effect of my abortive action was disastrous: Mr. Vale fell silent, stopped mopping his forehead and bent over to get a better look at what I had wanted to hide from him.

"'A Solution to Beauregard's Wild Number Problem,'" he read aloud, "'by Isaac Swift.'"

Dimitri glanced at me with arched eyebrows, waiting for a cue; when I shrugged resignedly, he turned to Mr. Vale. "Can you keep a secret?"

Mr. Vale had resumed mopping his forehead, more agitatedly now. "Can I keep a secret? Can I keep a secret?" he panted. "I cannot believe my eyes or my ears, Professor Arkanov. It was I who showed your esteemed colleague the solution to the Wild Number Problem less than three weeks ago!"

"Let me reassure you, Mr. Vale," I said. "My solution does not bear the slightest resemblance to yours."

"I am sure it doesn't," he said with a contemptuous laugh. "You have had three weeks to disguise my work beyond recognition while leaving the core of the argument intact. Brilliant, Professor Swift, positively brilliant."

"Come, come, Mr. Vale," Dimitri chuckled, "You know as well as I do that Isaac wouldn't stoop so low."

"Do I? Do you? Mathematicians all over the world have been searching for the answer to this problem for over a hundred and fifty years. Tell me, Professor Arkanov, do you not find it a trifle peculiar that all of a sudden, within a time span of a mere three weeks, in one and the same town, two solutions are found, completely independent of each other? A remarkable coincidence, wouldn't you say?"

"Why don't you judge for yourself?" I said, sliding my copy of the article towards the end of the desk.

One cursory look at the first page had him trembling with rage. "Does your audacity know no bounds, Professor? You are showing me my own work!"

I looked at Dimitri helplessly.

"Mr. Vale," he began, adopting his most authoritative voice and rising from his chair. "You have just made a serious accusation, a very serious one indeed. I trust you understand that we must treat this painful matter with the utmost discretion. The proper procedures must be followed. If, heaven forbid, it is true what you say, I assure you that the strongest possible disciplinary measures will be taken. But first I would like a word in private with Professor Swift to see what he has to say for himself. I am confident that all of this is just an unfortunate misunderstanding, and that everything will have been straightened out when you come in to see him tomorrow afternoon."

Several times Mr. Vale gasped for breath to continue protesting, but then he thought the better of it and let the air out of his lungs in a long, uneven sigh. "I do not share your optimism, Professor Arkanov," he said. "But if this is how we must proceed, so be it."

Dimitri placed a hand on his back and showed him out. In the doorway, Mr. Vale spun around to give me a final word of warning: "You may be thinking: 'It is a professional mathematician's word against an amateur's, so I have nothing to fear.' But mark my words, Professor Swift: justice will prevail! Justice will prevail!"

"We'll see to that," Dimitri promised, launching him into the corridor with a push of his fingertips and quickly closing the door on him. He returned to the desk and sank into his chair rubbing his eyes, fatigued by his diplomatic efforts. He picked up my article but put it down again, no longer in the mood for high abstraction.

"Justice will prevail!" came Mr. Vale's voice from down the corridor.

Dimitri and I stared at each other. Our grave expressions lost their stability and melted into laughter.

"I should have known this might happen," I said, wiping the tears out of my eyes. "What do we do now?"

"Let me worry about that. You go and mail your article before it causes any more trouble."

He accompanied me to the door. "Oh yes, I almost forgot to tell you: I had a word this morning with Daniel Goldstein. He is looking forward to receiving your manuscript and will do everything within his power to get it into the August issue." He noticed my eyes widening. "I told you I was going to call him, didn't I? Surely there is no harm in pulling a few strings for a just cause. The mathematical community deserves to hear the good news as soon as possible."

"It's not that I mind. It's just hard to believe all of this is really happening."

"And this is only the beginning," Dimitri laughed, patting me on the back. "I'll see you tomorrow then. Maybe we can take up the thread of our earlier conversation after we have sorted things out with poor Mr. Vale."

On my way to the administration, I had to pass Larry's office again. To avoid any further disturbances, I rolled up my article so that he would not be able to read the title.

He appeared to be totally absorbed in his work as I walked past his door, when all of a sudden he jumped up and yelled: "Justice will prevail! Justice will prevail!" Seeing the startled look on my face, he fell back into his chair cackling with laughter.

I did my best to appear amused.

"What was the matter with him anyway, besides the usual?"

"No idea," I was quick in answering, meanwhile fanning myself with my rolled-up article. "Maybe the heat got to him."

"You'd better watch out, Isaac. He might come back with a shotgun."

"I'll bear that in mind," I said, walking away before Larry could come up with another witty remark.

While I searched for an envelope and stamps in the cupboard of office supplies, I kept looking over my shoulder, almost expecting Mr. Vale really to be standing there with a gun aimed at me. In any event, it was safer to mail my article on the way home rather than to leave it with the administration. I made sure the coast was clear and went out to get my bicycle.

Leaving the campus grounds already made me feel better; two blocks later I broke into a smile upon spotting a mailbox. I kissed my article good luck on its further journey and then rode on, whistling a merry tune. Five plus three still equalled eight. Mr. Vale's outburst amounted to little more than a mosquito bite on an otherwise perfect summer's day. My article was on its way to *Number*, and there was nothing he could do to stop it.

My article was on its way to *Number*, the most prestigious periodical in my field! To be taken seriously by your fellow mathematicians, it is a definite must to grace its pages at some point in your career. Needless to say, Dimitri has been a regular contributor over the years; regrettably, Larry ranks second in our faculty–a distant second, to be sure, but no mean feat considering he is only twenty-nine years old ("I'll beat that old Russki in no time," he contends); a handful of my other colleagues have appeared once or twice. As for me, I had given up hope. When you are thirty-five, which is already quite old for a mathematician, and still "numberless" as we call it, you are well on your way to everlasting anonymity, never to be quoted and always to be seated somewhere at the back at conferences, assuming you manage to scrounge together the funds needed to attend in the first place. My solution to the Wild Number Problem had changed everything. It was late in coming, but I could not have hoped for a more spectacular debut.

This called for celebration. On my way home, I made a detour to the liquor store, where I bought a bottle of champagne to bring along to tomorrow evening's barbecue at Stan and Anne's. Stan deserved my eternal gratitude: he had helped me through my darkest moments and had persuaded me to show Dimitri what I was working on. I looked forward to his friendly punch in the shoulder, and to lovely Anne teasingly pressing her body against mine in a congratulatory embrace. I hoped Vernon Ludlow would be there, the know-it-all who at the previous party had claimed mathematics was a thing of the past. Or even Betty Lane, the embittered divorcee Anne had tried to set me up with. This time, I'd parry her cynicism with a happy shrug, much to her chagrin, no doubt.

> Anne and Stan, Stan and Anne
> from the jungles of the Yucatan
> to the mountains of Afghanistan.

I rode up the steepest part of the hill to the rhythm of these lines. They were the only ones I had come up with so far for my speech at their upcoming wedding. Like a catchy but ugly commercial jingle, they had come to haunt me on nights that I already lay sleepless because of the wild numbers. I now pictured myself at the wedding banquet, raising my glass to the bride and groom. Anne and Stan, I would say, pausing for suspense while looking at each of the guests in turn, Stan and Anne, half-closing my eyelids and beginning to smile. From the jungles of the Yucatan to the mountains of Afghanistan. Peals of laughter and an explosion of applause would be my due. Not that the lines had become any better, but I was now Isaac Swift, the well-known mathematician who had tamed the wild numbers.

Soon I was back in my apartment and the champagne was lying in the fridge. The wedding was a long way away, and the barbecue was not until tomorrow. Something had to be done to satisfy my immediate urge to celebrate, but I couldn't think of anyone to call. Kate, my ex, would not exactly appreciate hearing from me; my mother would not understand what all the fuss is about. "How very nice for you," she might say with that flat, cheerless voice of hers. My brother would no doubt be too busy with his kids. As for my father, since he and his new girlfriend had moved out west a few years ago, our contact had dwindled to Christmas cards and birthday greetings. No, better to let them find out by reading the *Chronicle.*

The *Chronicle*, or any other paper for that matter, national or foreign! The press normally takes no interest in mathematics: it scares people off, having been the cause of so much suffering in high school. Except for an occasional photograph of a fractal, which looks nice, or a sporadic reference to chaos theory, which sounds interesting, mathematics has been relegated to a corner of the puzzle page, for the amusement of those who wish to test their intelligence on a rainy Sunday afternoon. But my solution to the Wild Number Problem was real news, and could not be ignored. It did not matter that journalists would have a hard time explaining the problem to their readers–as long as people knew it was an important breakthrough, people like Kate and my mother, who kept nagging at me that I should abandon pure mathematics for something more practical and useful, like computers. What better way to silence these self-appointed critics than to have my name in the papers!

To blow off steam, I started cleaning up my apartment, the wild numbers having left little time for housekeeping. As I stuffed all the papers that were lying around in my study into garbage bags, I indulged in a fantasy of an international symposium held in my honor. I shook my head to dispel this delusion of grandeur, but was it really delusion? As Dimitri had said, the publication in *Number* was only the beginning. Invitations from faraway places would come pouring in, I would meet more people in the coming months than in the past fifteen years, and, now that I was not just a mathematician, but a famous mathematician, women would suddenly find me attractive, not just eccentric or at best amusing.

When I was through with my household chores, I still had energy left to burn. In spite of the oppressive heat, I went for my daily jog in the park. The hazy sky was painfully bright and the air was difficult to breathe, yet I flew over the path like an Olympic champion. I overtook a female jogger, her ponytail bobbing merrily up and down, and bounded past a group of teenagers slouched on a park bench, whose dark, challenging expressions would normally have disconcerted me. Farther on, I waved to a neighbor from down the hall who was trying his luck with a boomerang; wisely he had brought his dog along to retrieve it.

"Isaac Swift goes jogging every day," I thought, as if reading about myself in a magazine. "'It helps clear the mind,' he explains. 'Not many people realize how exhausting mathematics can be, physically as well as mentally. It helps to be in good shape.'"

I have always hated interviews with well-known people. Their success makes everything look so easy, their every move seems so purposeful. But as I ran through the park, I too was able to view everything in the light of my recent achievement. A sort of Copernican revolution had taken place. Before solving the Wild Number Problem, I had lived in a state of confusion, needing ever more desperate reassurances to explain away my erratic thoughts. Now, with my brilliant theorem shining in the center of my universe, everything fell into place. Even my most painful memories orbited neatly around the new-born sun, reflecting its wondrous light. My life had become as simple as five plus three.

Returning to my apartment, I had a long, cold, wonderful shower. Then I put on my bathrobe and went to the kitchen to make a pitcher of iced tea. "There is an awkwardness in his manner as he prepares drinks for us," I let my interviewer write, "But here in this sparsely furnished apartment, in the warm light of late afternoon, I sense that I am in the presence of a great mind."

"Isaac, Isaac!" I cried out loud, beating my fist on the counter. But like an amused parent, I couldn't help smiling at my mischievous imagination.

I spent the evening on my balcony. I had treated myself to a pizza to avoid the bother of doing groceries. Judging by the delivery boy's wide eyes and stammering words of thanks, he had never been tipped so generously. The empty box now lay by my feet. Sipping a beer, I watched the bats fluttering by, as unpredictable as the shreds of music and laughter that came to me from across the park. I was in the mood for making love, but my desire was as mild as the evening, and I was just as happy to sit back and enjoy the view. In the distance, the three white lights of the television mast flashed on and off, as did the two red lights, at a slightly slower rate. Since childhood, I have tried without success to tap the two rhythms simultaneously. I became so caught up in a renewed effort that it took me a while to realize that the ringing telephone was mine. I went inside to answer it.

"Professor Swift?" The voice was all too familiar.

"You know that you are not supposed to call us at home," I said sternly.

"The gravity of the current situation more than justifies this minor breach of etiquette," Mr. Vale replied. "Earlier today I was outraged, but as the day progressed, my anger made way for pity. How desperate your longing for success must be, to steal another man's work. I am not a religious person, professor, but I am tempted to pray for you. Yes, to pray that you will be granted insight into what a terrible mistake you are making."

"Mr. Vale, I can only reiterate what I said this morning. It is you who are mistaken."

"What foul demon has taken possession of your soul, inspiring you to such grotesque distortions of the truth? I plead with you, professor: listen to your conscience. Listen to the voice of reason."

"No. Now you listen to me. This conversation is pointless. I'll see you tomorrow in my office, all right?" I hung up without waiting for an answer.

No sooner had I stepped onto my balcony than the phone began to ring again. I let it ring this time. Mr. Vale was not going to spoil the perfect evening. It rang about fifteen times. The silence that followed lasted only as long as it took him to dial again. I suppose I could have gone inside to disconnect the phone, but I became intrigued by the complex pattern that was formed by the ringing telephone and the syncopated flashes of red and white from the television mast. I swung my feet onto the railing and went back to sipping beer.

"'Patterns. Mathematics is the love of patterns,' Swift explains. 'Some of my best ideas come to me on this very balcony, just by watching those lights.'"

2

He had first appeared in September, in my Algebra 101 class. Middle-aged and in a tweed suit, he was seated in the front row with an enormous leather bag under his desk, sorely out of place among all the kids in T-shirts and jeans who had come fresh from high school. Addressing me with so much deference in his voice that at first I thought he was poking fun at me, he asked for permission to tape the lecture. As I had no objections, he zipped open his leather bag and proceeded to set up an old-fashioned tape recorder on his desk. Already, some of the boys – and girls, of course, although as usual they were vastly outnumbered – were snickering behind his back. I feared a long year lay ahead, knowing from experience that so-called mature students often meant trouble.

I was just starting with the annually recurring formalities – listing the books we would be using, sending around a sheet of paper to get the students' names and addresses, announcing a tentative date for the Christmas exam – when he raised his hand.

"Pardon my presumptuousness, professor, and please do not take this to mean I doubt your good intentions, but here we are obediently taking down the date of the exam before even having asked ourselves 'what is algebra?' "

"I was hoping to get the technicalities out of the way first, Mr. . . ."

"Vale. Leonard Vale."

"Right. Mr. Vale. If you'll bear with me, we will come to your question shortly."

"Your reassurance warms my heart, professor, for it happens only too often that we go stumbling blindly down the so-called path of knowledge without ever stopping to contemplate the grander plan."

"Yes, I suppose so. Now as I was saying, the exam is planned for December 10."

A few minutes later, while I was introducing the first basic concepts of algebra, he raised his hand again. This time he wanted to know whether I "felt comfortable" with the continuum hypothesis.

"I'm sorry, Mr. Vale. I don't quite see the connection between the continuum hypothesis and what we are discussing now."

"Then allow me to explain."

"If you don't mind, I would rather you didn't. We have a lot of material to cover today."

"Of course, professor. You may proceed."

"Thank you." My sarcasm was lost on him, but some other students laughed.

Throughout the lecture, Mr. Vale raised irrelevant questions and enlightened us with his philosophical insights. We spent so much time "contemplating the grander plan" that I covered less than half of what I had planned for my first class.

Later that week, Angela Lasalle complained about similar problems with Mr. Vale. Other colleagues were to follow.

We checked with the administration. He had enrolled as a full-time student and had been one of the first to pay tuition. His high school diploma was older than mine but perfectly valid. In short, he had every right to attend our classes.

It was not only during the lectures that Mr. Vale was a nuisance. I had two exceptionally bright students, Sebastian O'Grady and Peter Wong, who liked to stay after class to discuss a wide range of mathematical topics with me, providing a welcome supplement to the rather tedious routine of teaching a first year course. At least, until Mr. Vale caught on and decided to join them. His bizarre non sequiturs quashed every thinkable conversation. He did not tolerate being ignored, however, becoming quite aggressive if one of us dared to question the relevance of his remarks. Soon after, I was sad to see my prize students leaving the classroom as soon as my lecture ended.

The teaching assistants complained that Mr. Vale spoke up constantly during the tutorials, confusing the class with absurdly complicated alternatives to the perfectly straightforward proofs that had just been demonstrated on the board.

He began calling us at home, even after eleven. “I am frightfully sorry to disturb you at this hour,” he would say, “but inspiration simply cannot be constrained by office hours.”

“Why don’t you just tell him to shut up?” Larry suggested to us during a coffee break. The first-year course he was teaching was to begin the following week, so that he had not yet been exposed to Mr. Vale.

“As if we haven’t tried!” Angela protested. “The trouble is that he thinks he is doing us all a favor. ‘I understand you would like to get on with the course,’ he said to me the other day, ‘but as a man of science I consider it my duty to share my thoughts with the rest of the class.’ You can’t reason with him. Just wait till Monday and you’ll see what I mean.”

“I’m looking forward to it,” Larry said.

The following Monday, Dimitri, Angela and I were having lunch in the cafeteria when Larry came in looking even more pleased with himself than usual.

“‘How to Silence Mr. Vale: Lesson 1,’” he grinned, setting down his lunch box and looking expectantly at each of us in turn.

“Oh all right,” Angela sighed. “Have a seat and spit it out.”

“The very first time Vale opened his mouth,” he said, “I warned him that I was not going to put up with any disturbances. He protested that he had every right to ask questions. I replied that his words made too little sense to qualify as a question, ergo, they formed a disturbance. I went on to inform him that faculty members had the right to bar disruptive elements from their lectures. That really got him steamed. ‘Don’t you dare call me a disruptive element, Professor Oberdorfer! I demand an official apology!’ I reminded him that an official apology presupposed an official complaint, which would have to be filed to the Disciplinary

Committee of the Board of Trustees. 'That's exactly what I'll do,' he said. 'The sooner the better,' I encouraged him, and told him how to get to the administrative offices. I swear, I have never seen such a red face. The veins on his forehead seemed ready to burst. He packed his books and that stone-age tape recorder he always lugs around with him and stomped out of the room. My students gave me a standing ovation."

With his story told, Larry pretended not to care how we were going to react: humming a Bach melody, he opened his lunch box and took out a sandwich, lifting up a corner to inspect the contents. "Tuna fish," he announced.

Dimitri was the first to speak. "Inviting someone to complain to the Disciplinary Committee is not exactly equivalent to silencing him. I think we have just been listening to 'How to Aggravate a Problem, Lesson 1.'"

"Oh come on. They won't take him seriously."

"I wouldn't count on that if I were you," Dimitri said, winking at Angela and me. "As a matter of fact, I'd say he has a pretty good case against you."

No complaint was ever filed, however. The same afternoon, we received a call from a certain Mrs. Vale Richardson. Her brother had come home in a terrible state. Could she please come and have a word with us.

Two hours later, Angela and I joined Dimitri in his office to welcome her. Larry had seen no point in attending and had gone to play squash instead. The poor woman, evidently unacquainted with the informal atmosphere of university, had dressed in her Sunday best and had splashed on far too much perfume. She planted her handbag on her lap and fiddled nervously with the straps as she spoke.

"I suppose I should have come to see you earlier, but everything was fine up till this morning. Leonard always comes home with wonderful stories–he thinks very highly of you all. You have all been very kind to him, considering...well, I am sure you have noticed that my brother is, how shall we say, a little funny in the head." Mrs. Richardson had to laugh at her own words. We did not dare join in, so that she ended up feeling silly and apologizing to us.

She told us the story of her brother's mental breakdown. Last autumn, after more than twenty years as a high school math teacher in the city, he had felt it was time for change. Attracted by the adventure and the high salary in compensation for the harsh winter, he had accepted a position at a school in Graham's Crossing, a mining town in Alaska. He had had terrible trouble fitting in. In the letters she received from him, he complained that his pupils poked fun at his formal language and were not at all interested in the mathematical puzzles he prepared for them, and that the only action in town was to be found in the local bars, but that the patrons would not accept a city slicker in their midst. So he spent most of his time at home. After a few months, the letters stopped coming. She began to worry and decided to call him. He said everything was perfectly all right now, he just hadn't had the time to write her. But his voice had sounded strange, evasive. Three weeks later, she received a phone call from the school. The janitor had found him early in the morning, standing in front of a blackboard full of mathematical equations, lecturing animatedly to an empty classroom. Mrs. Richardson had brought him back to the city, where he had come to live with her. Feeling a deep need to share his insights with kindred spirits, he had latched upon the idea to return to university. All summer, he locked himself up in his room with an enormous pile of books, getting ready for the academic year. Mrs. Richardson and her husband had been unable to talk him out of it, and so here we were.

"Have you considered seeking professional help?" Angela wondered.

"He becomes furious at the slightest suggestion that something might be wrong with him," Mrs. Richardson sighed. "The doctors tell me that as long as he doesn't pose a threat to himself or to his surroundings, he cannot be treated against his will."

"Thank God for that." Dimitri's words came from the bottom of his heart. Some thirty years ago, Soviet authorities had sent him to a psychiatric institute in Volgograd in an effort to cure him of his dissident thoughts.

"I know I ought to agree with you," Mrs. Richardson said, "but that leaves him in my care, and how am I to know what to do? Every morning when he goes to campus I keep my fingers crossed."

"We understand your predicament, but surely this cannot go on for much longer," I said. "Exams are coming up soon. I'm afraid your brother will have to face up to the fact that he isn't suited for university."

"I don't suppose there is a way to exempt him from writing them?"

Angela shook her head. "That wouldn't be fair to the other students."

"No, of course." The last glimmer of hope faded out of her eyes at the prospect of her brother failing the semester.

A long, painful silence followed, which was finally broken by Dimitri. "Something in your story has been puzzling me, Mrs. Richardson. If he was a high school teacher, he must already have some sort of degree."

"Oh yes. He has a bachelor's."

"A bachelor's?" Angela and I cried in unison. Then why on earth had he enrolled in first year?

"He feels he was blind for most of his life and now wants to retrace all the steps of his education, this time in the light of what he keeps calling 'the grander plan.' The first books he read this summer were from elementary school. He went all the way back to 'see Spot run' and two plus two equals four."

"I suppose that does solve our problem," Dimitri mused. "If he has a degree, he doesn't have to write the exams. Officially, he isn't even allowed to, or for that matter to be enrolled as a full-time student. You see, the government subsidizes us for every student who enrolls."

"Oh my goodness," Mrs. Richardson said, covering her mouth with her hand. "Does that mean he will be thrown out of university?"

Angela and I glanced at each other, not quite able to conceal our intense relief at the prospect of being rid of him. Dimitri, however, had a more humane alternative in mind.

"No, don't worry," he laughed. "He has every right to audit whatever course he wishes to. Of course, that does entail that he behave as an auditor, as a listener who keeps his questions and comments to a minimum. But tell me, do you think he would accept such a status?"

"Oh yes, professor," Mrs. Richardson said, nodding eagerly. "He has always attached great value to rules and regulations. I am quite confident that he will co-operate."

"Good. I will have a word with him then."

A few days later at a faculty meeting, Dimitri reported that Mr. Vale had accepted his new role as auditor, promising to keep quiet during and after the lectures and never again to call us at home. He had not let himself be silenced completely, however, being firmly convinced of the importance of his views. The net result of the negotiations was that in exchange for his full co-operation, he would be allowed to discuss his ideas during a fifteen-minute session every Friday afternoon with one of the staff members whose lectures he followed, at least, if we had no objections. What it boiled down to was that we would each receive one dose of Vale every eight weeks. It seemed a manageable price to pay for peace.

The frequency of the visits had to be increased to once every seven weeks when Larry refused to go along with the plan. "I wasn't hired to keep nutcases off the streets," he said. "I'm a mathematician, not a social worker."

Dimitri did not bother to argue with him, but Angela was indignant. "Good God, Larry! Fifteen measly minutes once every eight weeks to make a poor soul a little bit happier. I guess your heart cannot stand the strain of such an enormous sacrifice."

"It's a matter of principle," he replied coolly. "I wouldn't even give him fifteen nanoseconds. That man belongs in an institution. He might get some real help there, instead of being patted on the back by a bunch of naïve do-gooders."

To our relief, Dimitri's plan was a success, Mr. Vale proving to be an exemplary auditor: no more questions, no more phone-calls, just a "good morning professor" when he entered the lecture room and a "good day professor" when he left. But then, on Friday afternoon, he would come and visit one of us with a thick pile of papers tucked under his arm, smiling from ear to ear. To make up for his week of silence, he immediately began rattling away at a mile a minute. The best thing to do was to let the storm pass, occasionally muttering "how fascinating" or "yes indeed." This was not always easy. We mathematicians love truth and despise slipshod reasoning, let alone falsehood or downright nonsense. Mr. Vale's distortions of the truth were as hair-raising as a high school orchestra's rendition of a Mozart symphony.

Sometimes, when it was too much to bear, I would say, "That is incorrect, Mr. Vale."

"I urge you to take a closer look, professor."

"I'm sorry, Mr. Vale, but this really is incorrect."

"No!" he would say, with the clenched fists of a child who doesn't get his way.

"Oh yes, now I see. You're absolutely right. My mistake." Arguing was pointless. It was the price we had to pay for peace.

As the year progressed, Mr. Vale's supposed discoveries became more and more spectacular. Just after Christmas, he showed Dimitri the answer to an old problem in number theory: are there an infinite number of prime pairs, that is, prime numbers that differ by 2 (e.g. 5 and 7, 11 and 13, 71 and 73)? The answer, contrary to the expectations of modern mathematics, was no. He had proved there was a highest pair, p_v and $p_v + 2$, the index v standing for Vale. "It would take a computer over a hundred years to calculate the values of the Vale Pair," he told Dimitri, "but what counts is proving its existence, is it not?" But he had saved the best part for last. The Vale Pair flanked an even number $p_v + 1$, which could not be written as the sum of two prime numbers, thus refuting the famous Goldbach conjecture!

Angela was shown a new transcendental number v, the Vale Constant, which was guaranteed to reconcile quantum mechanics with Einstein's theory of relativity, and might very well earn him a Nobel Prize. He had calculated v to 500 decimal places and had presented Angela with a handwritten copy. Above the number, its digits neatly grouped in rows and columns, he had written: "For Professor Angela Lasalle. May my constant be your guiding light in these dark and troubled times." She hung it up in her office, among her children's drawings.

Because Mr. Vale seriously believed he was making major breakthroughs every week and we had given up contradicting him, he began to behave like a genius among lesser lights, walking around with the disdainful smile that Kate used to call the "mathematician's smirk."

In a way I deserved his scorn, for my work was headed absolutely nowhere. My last article had appeared in a minor periodical a year earlier, and entailed a tediously technical proof of a theorem too obscure to rouse anybody's interest. Mr. Vale's periodic visits provided a good measure of the state I was in, my self-contempt increasing in direct proportion to his self-esteem. While my colleagues still considered his visits a fifteen-minute joke, I found it increasingly difficult to contain myself. By the time he left my office, I'd be seething with impotent rage, blaming his nonsense for poisoning the rest of my day.

I even became jealous of the poor fool. I envied his enthusiasm, the sparkles in his eyes, that mad joy that had made Archimedes run naked down the streets crying Eureka! These marks of inspiration had been lacking for so long that I began to doubt ever having had them, other than in my dreams. What did it matter that Mr. Vale's high spirits were based on delusion rather than on mathematical truth? There was a truth far simpler and more powerful: he was happy and I was not.

Spring came. A full year had passed since Kate and I broke up. I had hoped that my work would benefit now that I didn't have to waste my energy quarrelling and I had the apartment all to myself again, but as yet there had been no signs of improvement. To help me out of my impasse, Dimitri gave me an assignment. I was to refine the so-called calibrator sets, which he had introduced to number theory. They could provide more insight into K-reducibility, another one of his innovations, which in its turn could throw light on a number of rather obscure problems in number theory. Not exactly inspiring, but like a pathetic dog I gratefully accepted the bone thrown to me.

Then came that Friday afternoon in May, now three weeks ago, that was to become the turning point in my life. It seemed a day like any other. I had been sitting in my office all day, gnawing joylessly on the bone Dimitri had given me and feeling sorry for myself, when, on top of everything else, in came Mr. Vale. It was once again my turn to sit through his fifteen-minute discharge of nonsense.

"Voilà, monsieur le professeur," he said, handing me a pile of papers and sitting down across from me. He folded his hands behind his head and tipped back his chair, observing me with the mathematician's smirk.

The pages crawled with incomprehensible equations in his familiar scratchy handwriting. He always threw in as many integral signs, sigmas and other mathematical symbols as possible, reminding me of the calculations of comic book geniuses. Here and there he had left a clearing in the dense jungle of formulae, in which he had written profound aphorisms, underlined three times and followed by three exclamation marks.

"Remarkable," I said wearily.

"What, professor, what is it that you find remarkable?"

This was a new tactic: rather than accepting our compliments, he would put us to the test, forcing us to admit ignorance.

"I'm not quite sure."

"Come now, professor. You can do better than that."

Though based on erroneous assumptions, his words rang painfully true. It was as if Mr. Vale was a hideous manifestation of my own conscience.

I shrugged guiltily.

"You really should keep up with the literature," he instructed me.

And he was right; every night when I switched off the television after hours of gaping at unattainable beauties on MTV, I scolded myself for not having read the latest issue of *Number* instead.

"This happens to be my most spectacular result thus far," he went on to say. "Making use of the latest developments in chaos theory, I have found the solution to Anatole Millechamps de Beauregard's Wild Number Problem."

"Amazing," I said.

3

Since Beauregard posed the problem in 1823, it has enraptured scores of mathematicians and others, from leading scholars to misguided cranks. It was to be expected that Mr. Vale would come up with a solution one day. Yet I could not prevent his newest achievement from touching a raw nerve. More than any of my unsuccessful projects, the Wild Number Problem reminded me of the dreams that I had given up.

I first came across Beauregard and the wild numbers when I was sixteen, while leafing through various mathematics encyclopedias in the library. It was a beautiful problem, but I was already sufficiently versed in mathematics to understand that years of study were needed to have anything sensible to say about the subject. The answer would probably remain out of my reach, but I did hope to make a modest contribution towards finding one somewhere in the distant future. At least as fascinating to me as the numbers themselves was their inventor. While my peers were worshipping their rock stars, Beauregard became my idol. I even made a photocopy of a famous portrait of him that I found in a book. Although the copy turned out rather dark, it hung on my bedroom wall for several months.

Anatole Millechamps de Beauregard was born in Amboise, France, in 1791. His mother died in childbirth and his father, a wealthy landowner, soon after, leaving him with an enormous inheritance and in the care of a governess. He soon proved to be one of those prodigies who can speak fluent Latin and Greek by the age of six. With his voracious appetite for knowledge and his instant grasp of new concepts, he drove a long string of tutors to despair. "Within weeks I had nothing left to teach him," one of them wrote in his memoirs. "His mind was like a spreading forest fire, consuming everything in its path." Mathematics was his greatest passion. He had soon read all the great works and threw himself upon the open questions of his day. In a mere afternoon, the seventeen-year-old Anatole resolved the Archipelago Paradox, which dated back to Ancient Greece and had confounded scholars ever since.

The ease with which he made this beautiful discovery filled me with awe. I had to slave away for hours even to understand existing mathematical principles, let alone to come up with something new.

But although his mathematical intuition was unrivalled, Beauregard was too restless to dwell on a matter for very long. With more discipline he would have ranked among the greatest, historians agree. As it was, his contribution to mathematics remained limited to a few isolated potshots. "Finding an answer invariably saddens me," he once confided to a friend. "The very moment I embrace mystery, it turns commonplace and banal."

In his continuing battle against boredom Beauregard made up a gambling game with a circle of friends: he would pose a mathematical riddle, everybody deposited a sum of money, and whoever solved the riddle took the jackpot. If after a given period of time the answer had not yet been found, the stakes were raised. Many of the riddles were diophantine problems, the type in which cows, goats and chickens have to be transported across rivers. Some were exceedingly silly, like "What makes the set {1, 2, 3, 4, 5, 6, 7, 8, 9, 10, 11, 12, 13, 15, 16, 20, 30, 100, 1000} unique?" (The answer: it contains all numbers that are monosyllabic in French.) Others were more profound and are still cited in lectures today, such as the question of how five balls bouncing inside a cube move in relation to each other (in keeping with his hobby, Larry has christened it the Squash Ball Problem). If his friends gave up, which was often the case, Beauregard would win the jackpot. Not that anybody minded, for he used his winnings to finance the many wild parties he held in his country mansion.

Contrary to the popular image of the mathematician as a withdrawn and unsociable being, Beauregard had a magnetic personality, and his appetite for wine, women and song was as great as for knowledge. There was hope for me yet, at least, so I thought as a lonely adolescent, as I admired his smiling portrait on my bedroom wall. "Anatole drank people with his eyes in the same way that he downed a glass of wine," one friend recalled. "Everybody fell in love with him, men and women alike. They could not help but open like flowers in the brilliant sunshine of his presence, revealing their innermost secrets to him." But as with mathematical problems, once he found out what these secrets were, he immediately lost interest. "It takes me an evening to decipher a man, a night to decipher a woman," he is reported to have said.

The nonchalant manner in which he cast people aside ultimately became his downfall. Warned by a jealous ex-mistress, one of Beauregard's closest friends caught him in bed with his wife. Blind with rage, he strangled them both. Because this was clearly a crime of passion, the betrayed husband was acquitted of murder.

Beauregard's death at the age of thirty-two left one of his mathematical riddles unsolved. To honor his memory, some of his friends, calling themselves "Les Amis de Beauregard," kept the betting tradition alive. Anybody who wished to join was required to pay a monthly sum. The riddle, which soon came to be known as the Wild Number Problem, originally wasn't much more than a tricky arithmetical problem. Beauregard had defined a number of deceptively simple operations, which, when applied to a whole number, at first resulted in fractions. But if the same steps were repeated often enough, the eventual outcome was once again a whole number. Or, as Beauregard cheerfully observed: "In all numbers lurks a wild number, guaranteed to emerge when you provoke them long enough." 0 yielded the wild number 11, 1 brought forth 67, 2 itself, 3 suddenly manifested itself as 4769, 4, surprisingly, brought forth 67 again. Beauregard himself had found fifty different wild numbers; the money prize was now awarded to whoever found a new one.

This was not as easy as it looked: the higher the initial number, the more complicated the calculations became, and with everything in those days having to be carried out by hand, the risk of error was enormous. Moreover, certain numbers, notably prime numbers, proved extremely difficult to "provoke." And when at last a wild number did reveal itself, it was usually one that had come up before, like 67. Thus, after months of lonely searching, many a disappointed number-hunter had to start all over again with a new initial number. I understood how frustrated they must have felt after I once foolishly attempted to find the wild number hidden in 103, which no one had ever yet managed to do. Armed with a calculator I launched an attack, but after an all-night struggle that left me with pages and pages of fractions but still no wild number, I conceded defeat.

Sometimes years went by before a new wild number was found. As the money in the jackpot accumulated, the problem attracted a growing number of people with little knowledge of mathematics. Besides such bounty-hunters, types like Mr. Vale appeared on the scene. Thus, the Friends of Beauregard were pestered for many years by a man who insisted he had found two wild numbers hidden inside the same number.

Not everybody was charmed by the problem. The English mathematician Alistair Beardsley (1800–1868) fulminated against it in his pamphlet "Wild Numbers and the Putrefaction of Mathematics":

> I suppose we should be grateful to the calculating brutes for locking themselves up in their gloomy dens, for we no longer run the risk of encountering them on the streets; but any mathematician who devotes his time to so trivial a problem is a disgrace to his profession. We can only pray that some day it will be proved that there are but a finite number of these thoroughly distasteful integers, the fewer the better, so that this barbarism can be left behind once and for all.

Unwittingly, Beardsley had raised a fundamental issue: how many wild numbers are there? Are there a finite number that keep coming up, and if so, how many, or are there an infinite number? A few years later, the Friends of Beauregard, swamped with supposed discoveries of new wild numbers that took weeks if not months to check, decided to call off the hunt, now offering the reward for an answer to Beardsley's question instead. A few zealots went on trying to find more wild numbers, but real mathematical know-how was needed to tackle the Wild Number Problem in its new form.

Some chauvinistic Britons rechristened it the Beardsley Problem, although Beardsley himself still believed it was unworthy of a true mathematician's attention.

It turned out he was wrong. Just like Columbus sought a new route to China and found America on his way, the methods that were developed to answer the Wild Number Problem led to all sorts of other discoveries, and more and more renowned scholars joined in the quest. The last remaining bounty-hunters lost interest in 1894, after one of the "Friends" had run off with the jackpot.

The first real advance was made in 1907, when the German mathematician Heinrich Riedel ended speculations that perhaps all numbers were wild by proving 3 was not: no number would ever reveal 3 as a result of Beauregard's operations. Five years later, he extended his proof to show that there were an infinite number of such "tame" numbers. It is still considered one of the most beautiful proofs in number theory, though also one of the most daunting ones. When I had a look at it as a second-year student, to my dismay I couldn't even follow the first step. If I ever wanted to work on the wild numbers, I had even farther to go than I had always thought. I comforted myself with the knowledge that most of Riedel's contemporaries had drawn a similar conclusion, abandoning their study of wild numbers and turning their attention to other matters.

For a long time after Riedel nothing much happened, apart from the usual rumors of imminent solutions which were subsequently never heard of again. Until in the early sixties, a brilliant mathematician in Moscow, none other than our very own Dimitri Ivanovich Arkanov, showed that there was a fundamental relationship between wild numbers and prime numbers, and that solving the Wild Number Problem would lead to a spectacular breakthrough in number theory. Dimitri's discovery was cause for great excitement in the mathematical community: the promised land would surpass the wildest expectations. Unfortunately, there was still no indication how to get there.

With the advent of computers that started around the same time, the hunt for new wild numbers was also reopened. Where Alistair Beardsley's "calculating brutes" would have given up, their eyes too bloodshot and their fingers too cramped to go on, the electronic brutes were just getting into gear. Every now and then over the past few decades, some proud team of computer scientists has announced that a new wild number has been found with the aid of an even more powerful computer. In 1981, for example, an unsightly, thirty-digit wild number was finally pulled out of the problem case 103. However, such successes threw no light whatsoever on the deeper mathematical question how many wild numbers there are.

But who in this day and age was willing to tackle such an excruciatingly difficult problem? Nobody in our faculty at any rate, as it turned out when we discussed the matter one day in the cafeteria. Dimitri felt he was too old to embark on the journey, youthful vigor was needed; the teaching assistants, representatives of the efficiency generation, did not want to risk coming out empty-handed after years of gruelling work, especially with the tight job market demanding quick results; Angela, genuinely modest, said she didn't have the capacity, while Larry found that the problem "didn't do anything" for him. Then it was my turn. As a latter-day Alistair Beardsley, I began to gripe about current policies and the decline of pure mathematics. While the government and the business community mindlessly pumped money into every silly computer project, we were constantly being threatened with cutbacks, the increased workload leaving no time for fundamental research.

Deep down I knew better: even with enough financial support and all the time in the world, I would not have started on the Wild

Number Problem anymore. As a sixteen-year old, I had dreamed of helping science a step closer towards a solution some day. But even this modest goal had been too ambitious. The problem was the exclusive domain of the great mathematicians, of the Beauregards, the Riedels, the Arkanovs. My mind was too awkward and sluggish; I lacked the imagination, the flair, the intuition to venture into a realm of such beauty.

Mr. Vale wasn't troubled in the least by such qualms that Friday afternoon in my office. Applying the Vale constant to chaos theory, he had proved there were an infinite number of wild numbers.

"Judging by the puzzlement that still clouds your features, I suspect these fifteen minutes have not been enough for you to plumb the depths of my reasoning," he said at the end of his visit. "But do not despair, professor. I will leave my findings with you. Study them carefully and patiently, and I assure you that the glorious truth will eventually dawn upon you, perhaps sooner than you think."

"That would be nice."

"And might I suggest that you store my findings in a safe place when you are done with them? We must not let this priceless knowledge fall into the wrong hands."

"Don't worry, I know just the place."

When he had left, I swept all his papers into a pile, eager to throw them into the wastepaper basket. Then it occurred to me that he might ask for them at a later date. It required an effort to suppress my distaste, but to avoid problems I stored them among my own papers in the top drawer of my filing cabinet. Then I tried to get back to work. I made a few uninspired notes on calibrator sets, but my thoughts began to wander, and soon the page was filled with doodles and geometric patterns.

It was then that something clicked in my head. I don't know

what prompted it, but all of a sudden I sensed that there was a deep, mysterious connection between the work Dimitri had assigned me and the Wild Number Problem. My intuition was immediately greeted by a storm of angry voices in my head. "You must be really desperate!" "Mr. Vale has infected you!" Loudest of all was Kate's voice. "Isaac, Isaac, when will you ever grow up?" she shrieked. I swore out loud and crumpled up the paper. Vague conjectures had never done me any good. After all, I was no Anatole de Beauregard.

I moved to the window. A student was sprinting across the field to his next lecture, his knapsack laden with heavy textbooks repeatedly hitting him full on the back. There went another eager young soul, thirsting for more knowledge. "Face it, Isaac, it's hopeless," a last voice said, before a deathly silence set in.

How the tiny, quivering flame of my intuition was able to withstand the numerous onslaughts of my doubts remains a mystery to me. It is the closest I have ever come to believing in God.

4

Not long after Mr. Vale had left me his so-called solution to the Wild Number Problem, I decided to pack it in for the day, having discarded my conjecture about wild numbers as pure folly. Yet another week had gone by, yet another weekend loomed ahead.

In the corridor I ran into Larry, on his way back to his office with a hot dog and a can of Pepsi. "You're off early today," he observed. “Going girl-hunting?” It was his own favorite pastime, in spite of a doting wife and a two-year-old son.

“How did you guess?” I said grimly.

“I don’t know about you,” he laughed, “but I certainly can’t concentrate with this fine weather. I’m trying to finish my article for *Number* before the weekend, but my balls have been doing all the thinking today.”

Bravo, Larry, I thought. Bravo.

When I came home, I stalled for an hour before finally changing into my jogging clothes and dragging myself to the park. I derived no pleasure from the exercise that day: it struck me as yet another neurotic attempt to run away from myself. After a few hundred meters I gave up and trudged back to my apartment.

There was a party that evening at Stan and Anne’s, but I was not in the mood and decided to stay home. After a makeshift dinner, I settled on the sofa with a beer and a bag of potato chips to watch the baseball game. The season was just getting underway; the standings were still full of zeroes and not enough players had been at bat yet to generate the vast quantities of statistics in which I liked to lose myself. The bare game failed to captivate me. One of the commercials in the first break featured a woman in a bubble bath, the rich foam only just concealing her breasts. Smiling dreamily, she dipped a sponge in the water and ran it along her arms, neck and shoulders. “Going girl-hunting?” Larry’s voice echoed, and I succumbed to the sinking feeling that I used to have in high school, home on a Friday night while everybody else was out having fun and sex.

Better times, when Stan and I went into town, were long gone. Thanks to his good looks and charm, girls always swarmed around us. I sometimes got lucky too, deriving my sex-appeal from his like the moon reflecting the light of the sun. And it was through him that I had met Kate. But when I emerged from my two-year relationship with her, I could no longer count on him for new adventures, his wild days being over for good. He was now a surgeon with a seventy-hour work week if not more, and he had met Anne, the girl of his dreams. They were engaged to be married and were planning to populate the numerous bedrooms of their new home with offspring. Stan and I still met every so often over a hasty lunch in one of the trendy cafés between the university and the hospital. Picking unhappily at our shrimp-filled avocados, we had to struggle to keep a conversation going. He listened to my rambling stories of inner turmoil nodding mechanically and stifling yawns. The inner peace that he had found did not make much of a story either. He seemed to have put his life on automatic pilot and was cruising comfortably towards old age.

Stan and Anne loved to share their happiness with their numerous friends. I don't know how they found the time, but they were constantly organizing parties. I hardly ever went, feeling ill at ease among the medical hotshots, the elegantly-clad co-workers from Anne's fashion magazine and all those other winners who spent the whole evening one-upping each other. The host and hostess patrolled back and forth between the various conversations to make sure everybody was having a good enough time. Anne especially kept a close eye on me. She was fond of me: I was Stan's Great Friend from the Past, and she would observe the two of us lovingly whenever we had a conversation, as if she were watching a home movie of her beloved's youth. Considering my bachelorhood an unacceptable state of affairs, she had taken it upon herself to find me a suitable mate. With a hand on my shoulder, she would point to various candidates among her guests, teasingly asking me which ones captured my fancy and why. These discussions with a gorgeous but unavailable woman were pleasantly erotic. They never lasted long, however, the hostess having too many other matters to attend to. She would lead me to a potential better half and with a few pleasantries pump up a conversation, which invariably fizzled the moment that she turned her back on us.

More than anything else, it was the prospect of watching yet another woman's smile fade with the word "mathematician" that kept me from going to the party that evening. I switched off the baseball game and reached for the entertainment section of the *Chronicle*, searching in vain for a movie that I might want to go to, then reading an interview with Shelley Sloane, the star of a "daring" new comedy series. Then I did part of the crossword puzzle. Three down: city in New Mexico (five, two). Six across: artless girl (seven). On the same page, there was a brainteaser: if it takes six lumberjacks six hours to chop down six trees, how many trees can sixty lumberjacks chop down in sixty hours? I was annoyed by all the tacit assumptions of the puzzle-makers. Didn't it depend on the thickness of the trees and the hardness of the wood? Didn't it depend on how much time the lumberjacks would waste arguing before getting themselves organized? As far as I was concerned, any answer would do.

All the sixes and sixties did turn my thoughts towards the Wild Number Problem again. "P_w," I scribbled in the margin of the page: the set of prime factors of wild numbers. If I could establish its K-reducibility with the aid of a suitable calibrator set... No, that wouldn't get me anywhere. "W_p," I wrote: the set of wild prime numbers. No. Damn. And yet there was a connection between the work Dimitri had assigned me and the Wild Number Problem. There had to be.

"No mathematics after dinner!" Kate would have said. Hastily I put down the newspaper and went back to watching the baseball game.

In the days she was living with me, I never knew when to stop working on a mathematical problem, often retreating into my study until two or three o'clock in the morning. Nauseous and dizzy, my head buzzing with complicated reasoning that led me around in circles, I would at last join her in bed, rolling around and heaving melodramatic sighs until she woke up.

"What's the matter, Isaac?"

"I can't find the answer. It's hopeless."

She would stroke my overheated forehead, telling me tomorrow was another day. Sometimes she tried to arouse me—making love worked wonders—but often I was too preoccupied to respond, deepening my sense of failure.

For my own protection, she made up the rule that I was not allowed to work in the evening. At first I complied, but as our relationship deteriorated, I became increasingly disobedient.

"And where do you think you're going?" she would snap at me as I wandered off after doing the dishes.

"I just want to write something down." When the idea turned out to be a dud, which was usually the case, I would spend hours and hours trying to find something else.

"Isaac, for God's sake come out of there!"

"I'll only be a minute."

Swearing loudly, she would go stomping off to bed.

Ironically, it was only after we broke up that she had her way. Lacking inspiration, I no longer felt inclined to work at home. It had been months since I last ventured into my study, and on that occasion I was only looking for a book for my student Peter Wong. In fact, the notes in the margin of the newspaper page were the first signs of after-dinner mathematical activity in over a year.

I stared at the W_p and the P_w that I had scribbled down, gradually sinking into a bog of muddled thoughts.

There you go again, Kate's voice chided me, *fleeing into mathematics because you're too chicken to go to a party!*

I switched off the television and went to get changed.

"Isaac, I'm so glad you made it!"

Anne threw her arms around me and kissed me exuberantly. Then she took me by the hand and led me into the living room. The party was in full swing, the guests standing in small circles with plates and glasses in their hands, their conversations whipped up by that nerve-racking sort of jazz that goes dribbling on and on without ever coming to a conclusion. I was led to a circle of colleagues from the fashion magazine.

"Girls, I'd like you to meet Isaac Swift. He's a mathematician." Anne swung around to attend to other guests, leaving me at their mercy.

"Good God," said a tall woman wearing a beret. "You mean you actually like that stuff?" She shuddered as if just having swallowed something horrible.

"You must be awfully brainy," said another. "I was terrible, simply terrible at math in high school."

The others just stared at me as if I were a zombie, the aforementioned brains oozing out of a crack in my skull.

I broke away from the unpleasant circle as soon as I could. In my student days, I used to do my best to convince my listeners of the charms and wonders of mathematics. I no longer bothered. Mathematics was an absolute turn-off at parties. Especially women disliked it, with a passion that I had given up trying to understand.

When Anne spotted me standing alone by the table with food and drinks, she grabbed me by the arm once more, now dragging me to a lone woman smoking in a corner, half-hidden behind a tropical fern. Her hard expression and dark clothing made her look like a young widow in mourning.

"Betty, this is Isaac Swift, Stan's best friend from university. Isaac, this is Betty Lane, my best friend from high school. And that's the doorbell." She ran off to answer it.

"So now we're supposed to be best friends," Betty said, looking me up and down with a sour look on her face. "Shall we start by swapping success stories, like all these other winners here?" In a tone devoid of emotion, she told me how she had given up a promising career in publishing to accompany her husband to Paris, where his software firm was sending him on a three-year assignment. Two months into their stay, he ran off with his twenty-year-old French secretary. No explanations, no apologies, just "You'll be hearing from my lawyer." And that was that. Three weeks ago she had taken a flight home. With no house or job, she had been forced to move back in with her parents.

"So much for my success story." She butted her cigarette in the earth of the tropical fern. "It's your turn."

It didn't seem proper to change the subject without first expressing my sympathy. Betty listened to my clumsy attempts with an almost triumphant smile: yet another inept reaction to add to her collection.

"Never mind," she said, deciding I had struggled long enough. "Just hurry up and tell me who you are."

I started telling her about my work at the university, but soon found myself talking to her profile.

"Would you rather I left you alone?" I asked her.

"Suit yourself," she shrugged, and lit another cigarette.

Not knowing what to do, I remained by her side watching the other partygoers.

"Well, what's keeping you?" she challenged me. "Go ahead and join the fun."

In order that Anne would not find me alone again and lead me into some new embarrassment, I sought refuge with Stan, who was crying shame upon the new tax laws together with a few of his colleagues.

Halfway through dessert, the beeper in his breast pocket went off.

"Oh no, not again," Anne groaned.

When he returned from the telephone, he was already halfway into his coat. "A traffic victim," he announced. "You'll all have to carry on without me."

"Party-pooper!" bellowed a ruddy-faced man who was having whiskey with dessert instead of coffee. "Get the ambulance to deliver the victim here. I'll bet there's more know-how gathered in this room than in the whole bloody hospital. We can move the salads aside and operate on that table over there."

"Hear hear!"

With an obliging smile Stan waved away the raucous laughter and left for the hospital, where he would probably have to spend the rest of the night in the operating room.

I would have gone home early had I not been trapped in a conversation by the ruddy-faced man, a gastroenterologist whose name was Vernon Ludlow. He advised me to abandon mathematics, it being a thing of the past, and turn my attention to computers.

"Artificial intelligence: now there's a fascinating field," he boomed. "And if I were you I would go commercial. You could easily be making ten times as much as at the university."

I tried to explain to him that computer science was intellectually less satisfying than pure mathematics, but I had derived so little pleasure from my work of late that my words lacked conviction. "I just don't want to stifle my thoughts to accommodate for the shortcomings of a machine," I heard myself say.

"My God, how arrogant can you get! Shortcomings? That's what life is all about. The great challenge is to overcome them, not to avoid them."

Just at that moment, his wife, a severe, emaciated woman, came by to hand him a new glass of whiskey. She nodded fiercely and gave me a dirty look before moving on.

"The trouble with you academics," he continued, poking an accusing finger into my chest, "Is that you have lost touch with reality. Of course, wouldn't it be grand if we could all sit up in our ivory towers spending other people's tax dollars to dream of abstract little wonderlands? But who would be left to do the real work? And who would pay for it? Huh? Tell me Isaac, what would happen if people in my profession refused to 'accommodate for the shortcomings' of the human body? Well? I'll tell you. The sick would die!"

I suppose I could have pointed out that his argumentation was faulty, but how was I to convince him of the value of my work, convince a doctor who saved people's lives? How was I to make a case for fiddling around with complex equations that only a handful of people understood? Instead, I listened resignedly to his whiskey-powered tirade against academics and other parasites of society and found myself more or less agreeing with him.

Anne rescued me from the one-sided fight. With her arm around my waist she led me aside to ask me a little favor. Stan had promised to drive Betty home, but now that he was at the hospital…

"No problem," I said, looking at my watch. "I was thinking of going home anyway."

"I didn't mean to chase you away. You will come back, won't you?"

"Well, it is getting late."

"But Isaac," she said, nudging me playfully. "What will people think about you and Betty if you don't return?"

When she had waited in vain for a witty answer, she became more serious. "She's just been through a horrible experience, but she's a wonderful person, you know."

The drive to her parents' house should have taken ten minutes, but Betty was terrible at giving directions and we became stuck in what seemed like a closed circuit of one-way streets.

"I knew I should have taken a cab," she grumbled when we arrived at the same intersection yet again.

We drove aimlessly through the slumbering residential neighborhoods. Past and future disintegrated, as if I had been stuck with this woman for an eternity and would be stuck with her for an eternity to come. I was dreaming of leaving her behind in the car and running off into the night, when she finally recognized a landmark and without any further problems directed me to the house.

"There's no place like home." She let out an uncontrolled bark of laughter that betrayed the pain lurking just beneath her cynical pose. "Thanks for the ride. It was great fun meeting you." She got out of the car, slammed the door and hurried up the path to the front door.

As I drove home, I felt old and depressed. There seemed to be no more room for dreams at my age. Everything was measured in terms of success and failure. The limit was no longer the sky, but the laughable contours of our flawed personalities and our deteriorating bodies.

Back in my apartment, I sank down on the sofa and switched on the television. There I was again, watching baseball, the newspaper full of senseless notes on wild numbers lying on the coffee-table. And there was the woman in the bubble bath again. I could just as well have stayed home all evening. Socially as well as mathematically, my life had come to a standstill.

For lack of any better ideas, I channel-hopped for a while, from a fifties melodrama in black and white via a news report on separatist fighting in a former Soviet republic to the rock videos of MTV. A discouragingly young man with a vacant expression that was probably meant to convey a great depth of feeling sang of love, while the camera zoomed in on a seemingly endless series of young women who kept vanishing from the screen before I could get a really good look at them.

In the next video, a bunch of dancers were engaged in frenzied acrobatics while a black girl with a baseball cap put on backwards invited the viewer to join the fun:

c'mon c'mon c'mon, I wanna see you move your bo-dy
c'mon c'mon c'mon, I wanna see you move your bo-dy

Even pressing a button to liberate myself from her obnoxious cheerfulness seemed too much of an effort.

c'mon c'mon c'mon, I wanna see you move your bo-dy

"All right all right I'll move my fucking body!" I cried, finally aiming the remote control at her and switching the television off. After staring at the blank screen for a while, I rose from the sofa and lumbered off to the bathroom to get ready for bed.

I don't know why, but instead of going straight to my bedroom after brushing my teeth, I opened the door to my study and went in. Lack of use had made the room musty, as if it belonged to a deceased person, the grieving family not yet having got around to clearing it out. I walked to the bookcase and reached for a thick volume on the top shelf: *Proceedings from the Third International Congress on Mathematics*, held in Edinburgh in 1912. On page 325

I found the article I was looking for: "Einige Bemerkungen über sogenannte zahme Zahlen," Heinrich Riedel's brilliant proof of the infinitude of non-wild, or tame numbers. Now if I could somehow refine Dimitri's sketchily outlined new concept of K-reducibility, then Riedel's proof might usher me into wild number territory.

It was miraculous. While on the surface I had wasted my time with television and an unpleasant party, deeper down my intuition had been pursuing a course of its own, slowly developing into a definite idea.

NO mathematics after dinner! Once again, I lost heart. How dare I dream of solving the great Anatole Millechamps de Beauregard's riddle to posterity, abusing Dimitri Arkanov's fine work to chase a megalomaniac fantasy? My isolated existence was making me lose all sense of measure. This was what must have happened to Mr. Vale during his lonely nights as a high school teacher in Graham's Crossing. Now I, too, was seeing all sorts of patterns in the chaos of my thoughts, a sure sign of incipient insanity. I left the book lying on my desk and went to bed.

I lay awake for hours, plagued by feverish images.

c'mon c'mon c'mon, I wanna see you move your bo-dy

The black girl with the baseball cap changed into Anne, dancing in her living room. She gave me a naughty look as her hands disappeared behind her back. She unzipped her dress, and with a few sexy wriggles, let it slide from her shoulders. I reached out to her, but the room began to spin, and I ended up behind the tropical fern, where Betty Lane regarded me with profound disgust as she took another draw from her cigarette. Then I saw Stan, his nose and mouth covered by an operating mask, looking up from his work with an amused expression in his eyes. The patient whose brain he was operating on sat up straight and adjusted his tie. It was Mr. Vale. Stepping down from the table, he picked up his heavy briefcase and left the operating room. Now he was walking down the corridor of the mathematics department. Now I was walking down the corridor. There was Larry, chatting with Vernon Ludlow. Going girl-hunting? they asked me. Back to Anne, dancing half-naked in her living room, then to Betty Lane...

c'mon c'mon c'mon

I rolled onto my stomach, fluffed up my pillow and punched it down again. I turned to lie on my side, then rolled onto my back and stared up at the ceiling. At last I flung the blankets aside. I marched straight to my study, sat down at my desk and opened the *Proceedings* to page 325.

No mathematics after dinner. No mathematics after dinner. No mathematics after dinner.

"Shut up!" I cried. The noise and welter of images vanished from my mind. The only sounds now were the soft ticking of a moth beating its wings against my desk lamp and my own heavy breathing as I strained to understand every step of Riedel's proof.

I opened the top drawer and took out a sheet of white paper.

"May 27, 3:15 a.m.," I wrote. "Given a wild number w..."

5

That first night, I set out in high spirits, following the path Riedel had cut into the flanks of the Wild Number Problem. The point that he had reached in 1912, his proof that there were an infinite number of tame numbers, served me as a base camp. From there, equipped with my specialized mountain-gear, that is, with Dimitri's new concepts, I could continue my ascent. Every step I took required my fullest concentration; now and then I had to stop to catch my breath, giving me a moment's rest to marvel at the wondrous mathematical landscape all around me.

It seemed like an eternity since I had last ventured into this realm with my undivided attention, free from voices telling me to turn back or urging me to hurry up and get something published. It was like a homecoming, a return to the happiest moments of my childhood, when every new insight made the world bigger and more mysterious, not smaller and more banal, as was so often the case nowadays.

Back then, even the simplest rules and techniques of arithmetic were a source of great joy. In second grade, for instance, Miss Wallace explained to us how to "carry a one" when adding very big numbers, like twenty-seven and thirty-five. When I came home that afternoon, instead of going outside to play (instead of going outside to develop my communicative skills, Kate would say), I went upstairs to my room to add. After adding pairs of numbers for a while, I tried adding three at a time and was delighted to discover that at a given point I had to "carry a two." I then decided to go all out, writing down ten rows of numbers consisting of nines only. Just as I had hoped, I soon found myself having to carry a nine, and another nine, and so on. My mother had to call me three times before I finally came downstairs for dinner. Later that evening, I stuffed a sweater into the crack beneath my door so that my parents would not see my light was on, wrote down twenty twenty-digit numbers and proceeded to add them. When I had completed and double-checked the sum, I would have gladly started on an even bigger one had I not been overcome with sleep.

During the Christmas holidays that year, I spent most of my time up in my room adding large numbers. My parents were once again going through what they called "stormy weather." My younger brother Andrew fled outside; I fled into the serene world of addition, soon too absorbed in my work to pay attention to the screaming, the slamming of doors and the leaden silences that followed. I was high up in the mountains, where my parents' quarrelling sounded as insignificant as the pounding and squeaking of a lumber mill deep down in the valley.

Subtraction, and "borrowing" ones, although presented to us as the opposite of addition and carrying ones, turned out to be much more difficult and subject to peculiar restrictions. Miss Wallace warned us that we were not allowed to take a bigger number away from a smaller one. When I asked her what would happen if we did, she hesitated before answering, a panicky look in her eyes. "Well, let's just say you get zero, all right?" Her answer did not make sense. How could five minus five equal zero and five minus eight equal zero as well? The difference of three couldn't just vanish into thin air. "Stop worrying so much about it, Isaac," she said. "Just let it be zero for now." Her reassurance only made me more anxious. There was no such thing as "for now" in arithmetic. If five minus eight did equal zero, it always had and it always would.

That evening, I gathered all my courage and asked my father the forbidden question: "How much is five minus eight?"

"Negative three," came his voice, God-like from behind the newspaper. He usually did not like being disturbed while reading, but to my delight he folded the paper and, writing in the empty space in an automobile ad on the back page, showed me that there were numbers lower than zero, numbers with a minus written in front of them. I was shocked and thrilled by this new insight. Zero was no longer the absolute bottom of the arithmetical world, but the portal to an arithmetical underworld. It made such an impression on me that when my father laid an arm around my shoulders and told me that he was going to live somewhere else for a while, the news didn't really register.

Five minus eight equalled negative three. Fifteen minus thirty-two equalled negative seventeen. I could not sleep that night, the depths below zero giving me vertigo. Drawn to the edge, at first terrified, I then abandoned myself to falling. I seemed to be sinking through my bed, my bed was sinking through the floor, the house was sinking into the ground, everything sank into the deep, dark world of negative numbers. And all of a sudden there was my father, in a magnificent purple mantle and with a crown on his head, waiting to welcome me to his new kingdom.

The insights that I was gaining into the Wild Number Problem twenty-eight years later were not as earthshaking as my first acquaintance with negative numbers, though only by a matter of degree. Every step I took, no matter how small, revealed new mountain-tops and unexpected canyons in the magnificent and bizarre region of mathematics first explored by Anatole Millechamps de Beauregard.

This was mathematics at its very best. Unlike in other areas of thought, where knowledge tends to increase gradually, in mathematics the transition from ignorance to understanding is instantaneous and absolute. Either you see it or you don't. But if you do, the new land presents itself in razor-sharp focus, its beauty so intense that you feel you have grown wings and are capable of flying. It is what makes mathematics so addictive. I would not be surprised if there was a biochemical correlate to these flashes of understanding, some kind of opiate that the brain releases into the nervous system every time they occur.

Even Kate, who had a strong aversion to the exact sciences, once experienced the ecstasy of a mathematical revelation. The night that it happened, we fell in love.

Stan called one evening to ask me whether I was interested in saving a damsel in distress. Kate, a good friend of his, was working on her Ph.D. thesis in psychology. Her supervisor had demanded that she take a refresher course in statistics. With the exam coming up soon, she was close to despair. Would I be willing to explain the basic concepts to her? "By the way," he said. "She's kind of cute."

"Cute" was not the first word that came to mind when I showed her into my study the next evening. One would expect some token of gratitude for a stranger offering his help, but instead, her dark eyes flashed accusing looks at me. While unpacking her books, she fulminated against striving for mathematical precision in the domain of human emotions. I was not given the chance to agree with her. Being a mathematician, I was automatically one of the bad guys. The statistical approach to psychology was so revolting to her that she was physically incapable of studying the material. It was masculine thinking at its very worst. Why did we men demand that something be quantifiable before considering it scientific? She had the answer: because we panicked when confronted with matters that defied order, and thus banned them from our world. And why did we panic? Because the most disorderly, formless matter of all was our own pent-up, fucked-up emotionality.

"Why don't you have a seat," I said, sensing that it was pointless to argue with her.

We read through the introductory chapter of her statistics textbook. She was obviously intelligent enough to understand the material, but whenever I introduced a mathematical symbol into my story, she suffered a violent allergic reaction.

"Sigma this, sigma that," she said, waving her arms in front of her face, "You keep assuming I know what you're talking about!"

"I'm sorry." I explained to her what a sigma was.

"That's not the way you were using it just a minute ago."

"Yes it is."

"Well, you weren't very clear, then."

And so the evening progressed. At three o'clock in the morning, in the middle of yet another one of my attempts to explain something, she threw her pencil down on the table.

"This is pointless. I'm sorry, but I guess I'm just too dumb for this fascinating field of yours."

"Of course you're not!" I cried, fed up with her obstinacy. "And by the way, I'm not particularly fond of statistics either."

For the first time that evening, she smiled.

"Now please: give it one more shot."

"All right. For your sake."

"Now look. First you make a column of these numbers, you see?"

She pouted her lip and would not look at me as I went on my with my explanation, but at least she no longer objected to every single step.

"And finally, to get the standard deviation, you add these squares, divide by *n*..."

"Wait wait, shut up for a second." She studied the figures on the paper with a painful grimace. "So what you're saying is: add up this column, divide by that *n* over there, and..."

What took place then was the miracle of mathematical revelation: in a single instant, her dark brooding expression turned into dazzling sunshine.

"I don't believe this! I actually get it!"

Having completed the climb, we threw down our heavy backpacks and wiped the sweat from our brows. We were now standing together on the mountain pass, marvelling at the mathematical landscape. When I saw the panorama reflected in Kate's eyes, I noticed for the first time how beautiful she was. The women I had been attracted to over the years had never understood my passion for numbers, leading me to the conclusion that love and mathematics were mutually exclusive. But now, my adolescent dream of being able to share what mattered most to me with a girl was coming true.

"Unbelievable," she said. "Is this all there is to it?"

I hoped she would not notice the clock on the bookshelf: it was past four.

"Give me some more raw data," she said hungrily. "I want to see if I can figure this out all by myself. And don't make it too easy."

When I handed her a new list of numbers, she beamed as if it were a precious gift.

I watched her fingers playing hopscotch on the calculator keys, watched the way she bit her lower lip whenever she scribbled down a result on the sheet of paper, the way she chuckled when the figures still added up after double checking them. She let her hand rest on my forearm whenever she wanted to know something, and as we looked through her calculations together I could feel the warmth of her cheek near mine. I wondered whether I could get away with a kiss. Later she told me that she had done everything to encourage me. But I didn't dare, and so she kept asking for new problems. We were still sitting at my desk when dawn began to glow through the curtains.

For the first time since that memorable night with Kate, dawn found me at my desk again. I was deeply content in spite of having made little progress. My various attempts to apply Dimitri's method to the problem had been far too reckless, as if I could reach the top by charging straight up the mountain. Every time, I came tumbling back into base camp, dragging an avalanche of mistaken notions down with me. But at least I now knew how not to go about it, and besides, my first inspired night in years was well worth a few conceptual bruises.

To unwind after the long night of hard work, I stepped onto my balcony. It was freezing cold, and my eyes, painfully dry from staring so long at equations on paper, were filled with soothing tears. Down below, a *Chronicle* van rounded the corner with screeching tires and went roaring down the deserted street. It was too early for distinct colors: the city was immersed in uniform blue-grey. Only in the distance, the lights of the television mast flashed red and white, red, white. Kate and I had stood here too, after that night, watching the city slowly come to life, holding hands, kissing.

Several hours later, I was awakened by the telephone. It was my mother, to see if I felt like joining the others on Sunday. This was a recurring ritual: Andrew, Liz and their two children had dinner at her house every Sunday, and once in a while she felt obliged as a mother to invite me too. Even more sporadically, I felt obliged as a son to accept the invitation. The get-togethers were awful: I had to put up with two spoiled brats screaming all evening, while the conversation of the adults–insofar as a conversation was possible–only consisted of long-winded negotiations between grandma and parents concerning which one of them would take which child where at what time. As usual I politely declined the invitation, and as usual my mother didn't insist.

Only when I had hung up did I feel how little I had slept. Five plus four equalled nine. Seventeen minus twenty-eight equalled negative eleven. But instead of clearing my mind, the arithmetical exercise made my head throb. During the few hours of sleep, all thoughts on the Wild Number Problem had congealed into a nagging headache.

In the bathroom mirror, I looked into the dazed eyes of someone who had been alone for too long. "Hello," I said. "Hello, hello." My voice sounded strange, as if it belonged to someone else.

Eating breakfast was a chore: the granola, advertized on the box as being extra crunchy, felt unpleasantly rough on my tongue and made so much noise inside my head that I set the bowl aside and settled for coffee. I was suffering from an all-too-familiar feeling: a mathematical hangover.

Even when I was a child, my mathematical sprees invariably ended in hangovers. On one such occasion, I had just discovered a mysterious relationship between the square of the sum of any number of variables and the sum of their squares. I was up in my room, diligently writing it down in neat form.

$$(a+b)^2 = 2(a^2+b^2)-(b-a)^2$$
$$(a+b+c)^2 = 3(a^2+b^2+c^2)-((c-b)^2+(c-a)^2+(b-a)^2)$$
$$(a+b+c+d)^2 = 4(a^2+b^2+c^2+d^2)-((d-c)^2+(d-b)^2+(d-a)^2+(c-b)^2+(c-a)^2+(b-a)^2)$$

Years later, I was greatly disappointed to find out that the only mystery lay in my unfamiliarity with certain mathematical laws, the triviality of the relationship being hidden by the inefficient way in which I had expressed it. At the time, however, I was so thrilled by my discovery that my mother was halfway up the stairs before I finally heard her calling my name.

"Isaac! For the last time: lunch is ready!"

"Coming!" My bladder was about to burst. One of my legs had gone to sleep, so I had to limp to the bathroom, where I managed to unzip my fly just in time. While washing my hands I saw myself in the mirror and was struck by the dazed look in my eyes, a look that was to accompany me into adulthood.

Downstairs, the light in the kitchen was painfully bright and my mother's voice sounded shrill and unpleasant. She had never understood my passion for arithmetic, but since my father had left us she had become highly irritable and found my preoccupation downright annoying. Without looking at me she handed me a peanut butter sandwich and then went back to preparing an apple pie. I took a bite, but it seemed as if the hand holding the sandwich as well as the mouth tasting it belonged to someone else. Absently I noted that the fluffiness of the bread was being transformed to sogginess, which in its turn dissolved into the stickiness and strong flavor of peanut butter. Meanwhile, great swarms of numbers and equations were buzzing in my ears.

Then we heard footsteps on the back porch. "I'm wounded!" My brother Andrew burst into the kitchen, rosy-cheeked and smelling of earth and grass. "I'm wounded!" Rolling up a pant-leg, he showed us his bleeding knee.

"My poor boy." With a tender smile my mother lifted him onto a chair and knelt down to dress the wound, Andrew all the while telling her of his many adventures in the park, stumbling over his words in an effort not to miss any details. My adventures in the realm of numbers paled in comparison. When she applied iodine to his knee, he winced just like we had seen cowboys do it in westerns. I admired his pain, so clear and simple compared to the confusion of thoughts and sensations that were battling for my attention. Jealously I watched him being rewarded with a band-aid.

After lunch I withdrew to my room to continue working on my new discovery. But I no longer derived any pleasure from what I was doing: my neck was sore, my eyes were red, the happy voices of Andrew and his friends just outside my window made me feel lonely. In an effort to smother these unpleasant sensations, I wrote:

$$(a+b+c+d+e+f+g+h+i+j+k+l+m+n+o+p+q+r+s+t+u+v+w+x+y+z)^2=$$
$$26(a^2+b^2+c^2+d^2+e^2+f^2+g^2+h^2+i^2+j^2+k^2+l^2+m^2+n^2+o^2+p^2+q^2+r^2+s^2+t^2+u^2+v^2+w^2+x^2+y^2+z^2)-((z-y)^2+(z-x)^2+$$
$$(z-w)^2+(z-v)^2+(z-u)^2+(z-t)^2+(z-s)^2+(z-r)^2+(z-q)^2+$$
$$(z-p)^2+(z-o)^2+(z-n)^2+(z-m)^2+(z-l)^2+(z-k)^2+(z-j)^2+$$
$$(z-i)^2+(z-h)^2+(z-g)^2+(z-f)^2+(z-e)^2+(z-d)^2+(z-c)^2+$$
$$(z-b)^2+(z-a)^2+(y-x)^2+(y-w)^2+(y-v)^2+(y-u)^2+(y-t)^2+$$
$$(y-s)^2+(y-r)^2+(y-q)^2+(y-p)^2+(y-o)^2+(y-n)^2+(y-m)^2+$$
$$(y-l)^2+(y-k)^2+(y-j)^2+(y-i)^2+(y-h)^2+(y-g)^2+(y-f)^2+$$
$$(y-e)^2+(y-d)^2+(y-c)^2+(y-b)^2+(y-a)^2+(x-w)^2+(x-v)^2+$$
$$(x-u)^2+(x-t)^2+(x-s)^2+(x-r)^2+(x-q)^2+(x-p)^2+(x-o)^2+$$
$$(x-n)^2+(x-m)^2+(x-l)^2+(x-k)^2+(x-j)^2+(x-i)^2+(x-h)^2+$$
$$(x-g)^2+(x-f)^2+(x-e)^2+(x-d)^2+(x-c)^2+(x-b)^2+(x-a)^2+$$
$$(w-v)^2+(w-u)^2+(w-t)^2+(w-s)^2+(w-r)^2+(w-q)^2+(w-p)^2+$$
$$(w-o)^2+(w-n)^2+(w-m)^2+(w-l)^2+(w-k)^2+(w-j)^2+(w-i)^2+$$
$$(w-h)^2+(w-g)^2+(w-f)^2+(w-e)^2+(w-d)^2+(w-c)^2+(w-b)^2+$$
$$(w-a)^2+(v-u)^2+(v-t)^2+(v-s)^2+(v-r)^2+(v-q)^2+(v-p)^2+$$

$(v-o)^2+(v-n)^2+(v-m)^2+(v-l)^2+(v-k)^2+(v-j)^2+(v-i)^2+$
$(v-h)^2+(v-g)^2+(v-f)^2+(v-e)^2+(v-d)^2+(v-c)^2+(v-b)^2+$
$(v-a)^2+(u-t)^2+(u-s)^2+(u-r)^2+(u-q)^2+(u-p)^2+(u-o)^2+$
$(u-n)^2+(u-m)^2+(u-l)^2+(u-k)^2+(u-j)^2+(u-i)^2+(u-h)^2+$
$(u-g)^2+(u-f)^2+(u-e)^2+(u-d)^2+(u-c)^2+(u-b)^2+(u-a)^2+$
$(t-s)^2+(t-r)^2+(t-q)^2+(t-p)^2+(t-o)^2+(t-n)^2+(t-m)^2+$
$(t-l)^2+(t-k)^2+(t-j)^2+(t-i)^2+(t-h)^2+(t-g)^2+(t-f)^2+$
$(t-e)^2+(t-d)^2+(t-c)^2+(t-b)^2+(t-a)^2+(s-r)^2+(s-q)^2+$
$(s-p)^2+(s-o)^2+(s-n)^2+(s-m)^2+(s-l)^2+(s-k)^2+(s-j)^2+$
$(s-i)^2+(s-h)^2+(s-g)^2+(s-f)^2+(s-e)^2+(s-d)^2+(s-c)^2+$
$(s-b)^2+(s-a)^2+(r-q)^2+(r-p)^2+(r-o)^2+(r-n)^2+(r-m)^2+$
$(r-l)^2+(r-k)^2+(r-j)^2+(r-i)^2+(r-h)^2+(r-g)^2+(r-f)^2+$
$(r-e)^2+(r-d)^2+(r-c)^2+(r-b)^2+(r-a)^2+(q-p)^2+(q-o)^2+$
$(q-n)^2+(q-m)^2+(q-l)^2+(q-k)^2+(q-j)^2+(q-i)^2+(q-h)^2+$
$(q-g)^2+(q-f)^2+(q-e)^2+(q-d)^2+(q-c)^2+(q-b)^2+(q-a)^2+$
$(p-o)^2+(p-n)^2+(p-m)^2+(p-l)^2+(p-k)^2+(p-j)^2+(p-i)^2+$
$(p-h)^2+(p-g)^2+(p-f)^2+(p-e)^2+(p-d)^2+(p-c)^2+(p-b)^2+$
$(p-a)^2+(o-n)^2+(o-m)^2+(o-l)^2+(o-k)^2+(o-j)^2+(o-i)^2+$
$(o-h)^2+(o-g)^2+(o-f)^2+(o-e)^2+(o-d)^2+(o-c)^2+(o-b)^2+$
$(o-a)^2+(n-m)^2+(n-l)^2+(n-k)^2+(n-j)^2+(n-i)^2+(n-h)^2+$
$(n-g)^2+(n-f)^2+(n-e)^2+(n-d)^2+(n-c)^2+(n-b)^2+(n-a)^2+$
$(m-l)^2+(m-k)^2+(m-j)^2+(m-i)^2+(m-h)^2+(m-g)^2+(m-f)^2+$
$(m-e)^2+(m-d)^2+(m-c)^2+(m-b)^2+(m-a)^2+(l-k)^2+(l-j)^2+$
$(l-i)^2+(l-h)^2+(l-g)^2+(l-f)^2+(l-e)^2+(l-d)^2+(l-c)^2+$
$(l-b)^2+(l-a)^2+(k-j)^2+(k-i)^2+(k-h)^2+(k-g)^2+(k-f)^2+$
$(k-e)^2+(k-d)^2+(k-c)^2+(k-b)^2+(k-a)^2+(j-i)^2+(j-h)^2+$
$(j-g)^2+(j-f)^2+(j-e)^2+(j-d)^2+(j-c)^2+(j-b)^2+(j-a)^2+$
$(i-h)^2+(i-g)^2+(i-f)^2+(i-e)^2+(i-d)^2+(i-c)^2+(i-b)^2+$
$(i-a)^2+(h-g)^2+(h-f)^2+(h-e)^2+(h-d)^2+(h-c)^2+(h-b)^2+$
$(h-a)^2+(g-f)^2+(g-e)^2+(g-d)^2+(g-c)^2+(g-b)^2+(g-a)^2+$
$(f-e)^2+(f-d)^2+(f-c)^2+(f-b)^2+(f-a)^2+(e-d)^2+(e-c)^2+$

$(e-b)^2+(e-a)^2+(d-c)^2+(d-b)^2+(d-a)^2+(c-b)^2+(c-a)^2+(b-a)^2)$

It was the longest formula I had ever made up, but so what? Now my hand was sore and the buzzing in my head was worse than ever. To keep myself occupied, I picked twenty-six numbers and checked if the formula worked.

The variables in our family life may have changed as time passed, the basic equations remained the same. Thus, on the Saturday after a high school dance that I had not attended, I was once again up in my room, now in the middle of integrating a highly complex trigonometric function, when Andrew threw open the door.

"Guess what?" he said. "Penny and I went all the way last night."

"Good for you," I said without looking up from my work.

He had seen her home after the dance. With her parents out of town for the weekend, they had the place all to themselves. Right in the middle of the living room they had undressed each other. "And when we were completely naked–boy were we horny–then Penny lay down on the rug..."

"Would you mind keeping your animal exploits to yourself?" I snapped at him. "Can't you see I'm busy?

"God, you're an asshole." He turned and left my room, slamming the door behind him. "'Animal exploits,'" he cried from out in the hall. "You're just jealous, that's all."

Several hours later, I finally solved the problem, but the landscape that revealed itself had never seemed so barren and lifeless. Far more vivid was the image of Penny and my younger brother rolling around naked on a carpet. I had not even come close to a first kiss. Hastily, I made up a new problem, twice as complicated as the previous one. But I could not concentrate: the erotic images kept getting steamier. The portrait of Beauregard hanging on my wall offered me no solace that day. He had the same twinkles in his eyes and the same lecherous smile as my brother. And he was a brilliant mathematician to boot! Disgusted with my childish hero worship of the past few months, I tore the portrait from the wall.

As I grew older, I began to wonder whether mathematics really was a passion and not an addiction, a painkiller to dull the ache of unfulfilled desires. The pleasant effects of doing mathematics were gradually weakening, so that ever greater doses were needed, draining all the energy and healthy longing out of me. Was it love or compulsion that made me major in mathematics at university and later choose it as my profession?

To Kate the answer was obvious.

It was in the period that she was living with me that my career began to stagnate. My thesis, a detailed study on Templeton functions with countless openings for further research, had got me the job at the university. But even mathematics is subject to changing fashions, and of late everybody seemed to be losing interest in my area of research. Meanwhile, a former teaching assistant of mine, five years younger than me, had submitted his first article to *Number*. His name: Larry Oberdorfer. When he received the letter of acceptance from the editors, he spent the rest of the day roaming about in the hall. “It’s a bird! It’s a plane!” he would cry, and then jump into a colleague’s office with his arms outstretched. “It’s Numberman!”

Although Dimitri insisted that dwindling interest in Templeton functions was a matter of plain bad luck, and Angela warned me not to let myself be intimidated by Larry, I blamed myself for my lack of success: I had not worked hard enough to show the world the value of my work.

In a last-ditch effort, I persuaded Kate to waive the rule "No mathematics after dinner," promising her that my nightly sessions would only be temporary. After weeks of hard work, I was finally close to a publishable result. I had found a theorem which I knew with certainty to be true, but working out the details of the proof required an enormous amount of patience and mathematical technique. There was little reason to celebrate, for I knew in advance that the final result would be too meagre for *Number*. And it was unlikely to rekindle anybody's love for Templeton functions. Was it worth the bother? I needed all the powers of mind and body to motivate myself. Meanwhile Kate was losing her patience, nagging at me that we never went out anymore, that I was distant, that locking myself up like this was unhealthy.

To appease her, I agreed to go out that next Friday night. The world-famous Deirdre Lindsay Dance Company, which of course I had never heard of, was in town. Before the performance, we went to a fancy restaurant. Throughout dinner, we talked about our relationship, that is, Kate talked about me and I listened. Templeton functions were still buzzing in my head, making it difficult to concentrate on what she was saying, let alone to defend myself.

She had come to the conclusion that I was using mathematics as an escape, as a means to hide from my deeper feelings. I stared at her glassily while she stroked my hand and looked into my eyes with a warm, concerned expression.

"I don't think you have ever stopped to realize how hurt you were as a young child, when your parents got divorced. All you did was go up to your room to add and subtract."

I nodded. Mathematics was a drug, a painkiller. I had thought of that years ago.

"And I don't think you've ever come to terms with your being jealous of Andrew. He got your mother's love, he scored with the girls..."

Yes. That made sense too. If only the noise in my head stopped.

"And now you're upset by Larry publishing an article in *Number*. Don't you see the connection?"

I shook my head.

"Larry is your younger brother Andrew all over again."

This time, I felt compelled to react. "Don't be ridiculous!"

Kate smiled and stroked my hand some more. "I hate to play that old psychologist's trick on you, but if it isn't true, then why are you reacting so emotionally?"

"Because you're not being fair."

"Isaac. I am not an adversary. I am only trying to help you. I have a feeling that there is a wealth of emotions that you left behind in your childhood. I know they're inside you somewhere. You can be a very warm and loving person. But you keep shutting yourself off, retreating into the safe, orderly world of abstraction."

"So what do you want me to do? Give up mathematics?"

"Isaac!" she said reproachfully, but I didn't get a real answer.

She continued with her analysis of my personality during dessert and coffee. The more she picked me apart, the warmer her expression became. When it was time to go to the ballet, she was deeply in love with me again.

"I am so happy we finally talked, Isaac," she said, locking her arm in mine as we crossed the street towards the theater. "Aren't you?"

"Uh-huh."

When the lights in the theater were dimmed, she leaned towards me and gave me a passionate kiss. Deirdre Lindsay and her dancers began to prance about on the stage. "No story, no hidden meanings," according to the program, "just an ode to life, natural and pure." But I was left unmoved by what I saw, except for being mildly annoyed by the artificiality of the dancers' smiles. Kate held her hand in mine, our fingers interlaced. Two flaps of human flesh, I thought. Suddenly, the buzzing in my head became louder. If I switched around two steps in my proof, not only would it be greatly simplified, the implications of the theorem would be much farther-reaching! If only I had pen and paper to write it all down. I prayed that I could hold onto my thoughts. I could already feel them slipping away.

In the intermission, I excused myself and hurried to the washroom. Locking myself in one of the cubicles, I groped around in the inside pocket of my jacket and found a pen, yanked a strip of toilet paper from the roll and wrote down as much as I could remember. Switching the steps around was not as easy as I had thought. *$f'(x)$ is an element of, $f'(x)$ is an element of...* The gong sounded. Damn! I flushed the toilet and stepped out of the cubicle. Several men by the urinals turned and stared. I wiped the sweat from my forehead with the toilet paper full of notes, then stuffed it into my pocket.

"Isaac, are you all right?" Kate asked me. "You were in there for an awfully long time."

"I'm fine. I'm fine."

While Deirdre Lindsay and her troupe went on celebrating life, I tried with all my might to focus on Templeton functions. Kate didn't make it any easier: she had placed her hand on my crotch and was giving me little squeezes there. I shifted in my chair.

"Scaredy-cat," she whispered, nibbling on my earlobe. "Just wait till we get home."

Sure enough, when we got back to the apartment that night she led me straight into the bedroom, where she pinned me against the wall and started kissing me wildly. Her tongue probing deep into my mouth left little room for mathematical reflection. She unbuttoned my shirt and stroked my chest, then unzipped my fly and pulled down my pants. My body responded to her hands and lips as it should; as my desire swelled, all thoughts on Templeton functions shrank back into the farthest corners of my mind. I now undressed her too. We tumbled onto the bed, and for a while we made love with at least as much passion as in the early days, until something strange happened: all of a sudden I was working on Templeton functions again, meanwhile looking down upon the rhythmic movements of our two bodies. My thoughts became irritatingly synchronized with my sensations: every kiss or caress, every groan or thrust corresponded to a step in my proof, but the repetitiveness of our motions prevented me from reaching the desired result. Only through Kate's body could I get to the unknown on the other side of the equation, but I could not penetrate her deep enough: $f'(x)$ is an element of T if and only if, if and only if, $f'(x)$ is an element of T if, if if, if and only if... The incomplete step repeated itself faster and faster until we reached our climax.

While Kate lay in my arms catching her breath, I stared up at the ceiling. Of course: $f'(x)$ is an element of T if and only if there is a number N such that for all x greater than N, $f'(x)$ is Templeton-continuous. So the next step was to prove that there was such a number N.

"Isaac," Kate said, interrupting my train of thought. There was a languid, dreamy look in her eyes.

"Huh?"

"See what happens when you don't work on mathematics in the evening?"

"Yes."

"See how passionate it can be?"

"Uh-huh."

She fell asleep in my arms. I was wide awake, now only a few minor steps away from cracking the problem. But I would have to get to my study, to pen and paper. Ever so carefully, I lifted her limp arm from my chest and let it fall onto the pillow. She made some smacking sounds with her lips, rolled over onto her other side and went on sleeping. I got out of bed, swept up whatever garments I could find in the dark and tiptoed out of the room.

Soon I was sitting at my desk, wearing pants but no shirt and only one sock. Kate's dress, accidentally brought along too, was now hanging over the chair across from me. At first I cast anxious looks at the door, but then I squared my shoulders and gave the Templeton-functions my full attention. Alas, hours of meticulous work ended in deception: there was nothing to be gained from switching around two steps in my proof.

I stared at Kate's dress. She had not even noticed how distant I was during our lovemaking. On the contrary, she thought we had never been so close. Her passion and tenderness had been wasted on me, all because of a bunch of silly mathematical equations. In a delayed reaction, I was flooded with warm feelings toward her.

With tears in my eyes and determined to make more of an effort in the future, I crept back into bed and curled up against her. I wanted to make love to her again, this time with my undivided attention. I laid my hand on her thigh and kissed her shoulder repeatedly, but she was too fast asleep to respond.

It was the last time we came close to being close. The next morning while I was still sleeping, Kate found her dress in my study. Puzzled and upset, she woke me up. When I had confessed my crime she was furious, as if just having found out that in spite of assurances to the contrary, I was still seeing some other woman.

Hangovers. The morning after my all-night wild number binge, my life seemed like a long string of hangovers, with precious little in between.

Wistfully dredging up spoonfuls of granola and letting them fall back into the bowl of milk again, I wondered what had got into me last night. My addiction seemed to have moved into a new, more dangerous phase. In the past, I may have worked far too hard and far too long on a problem, but never had I tackled anything that lay beyond the limits of my mathematical ability. I had always been a prudent mountaineer, knowing exactly which rock faces and ice fields to avoid before setting out on an expedition. Now I had charged straight up the mountain like a raving lunatic.

In retrospect, I am glad to have let go of the conservative estimate of my capacities that night. Without reaching for the stars, I would never have found the solution to the Wild Number Problem. But it is always easy to congratulate yourself for taking risks after they have paid off. At the time, I was panic-stricken.

I went to my study, determined to throw away all the deluded scribbling of the night before. While cleaning up my desk, however, the buzzing in my head became louder, compelling me to sit down again.

All day Saturday and all day Sunday I went on working. Patching up my temporary assumptions with more temporary assumptions, the load that I had to carry up the mountain became heavier and heavier. I begged myself to give up. I briefly considered going to the family dinner after all, then settled for a walk in the park to get the wild numbers out of my system. But the sun was too bright, I was frightened by the people around me, and they seemed just as frightened by me. As usual, the withdrawal symptoms were worse than the drug itself. I went hurrying back to my study for the only remedy that I had ever known: a new and stronger dose of mathematics.

In spite of having a class to teach at nine, I was still working on the problem at four in the morning. The mathematical landscape around me had become oppressive and menacing. Nothing made sense anymore. This region had never been explored by Anatole Millechamps de Beauregard, the path that I was following had not been cut by Heinrich Riedel, the mountain gear that I was using had not been designed by Dimitri Arkanov. Nor did this path lead to truth. It led in exactly the opposite direction.

Only one other person had ventured here before me. He was my guide and was walking just ahead of me, carrying his old tape recorder.

6

Three hours of troubled sleep carried me from my wild number weekend into Monday morning. If it had not been for my responsibility as an educator I would have called in sick: the very last algebra class before the final exam was at nine, and my students would undoubtedly have a lot of questions to ask me. Avoiding the strong gravitational field of my study, where the Wild Number Problem lay waiting to pull me in, I continued to the bathroom. Although I was expecting the worst, my mirror image still came as a shock. Framed by wild hair and a three-day beard, my eyes burned with the feverish luminosity of a religious fanatic.

When I had washed and shaven, I had a hasty breakfast and left for the university far earlier than necessary, hoping that the cool professional atmosphere of my office would help restore my calm.

Finding myself on my bicycle in the surge of rush-hour traffic already had a soothing effect on me: after a lonely and mad weekend I was once again a citizen among citizens, clean-shaven and on his way to work, stopping for red lights and continuing on green.

When I got to the university, however, my gradual return to normalcy suffered a serious setback. As I entered the long corridor, I spotted Mr. Vale waiting outside my office. All year, he had abided by the rules, keeping quiet in class and never bothering us outside the weekly fifteen-minute sessions. Why had he picked this particular morning to break them? And why had he chosen me as his victim? It could not be coincidence. He had brought up the Wild Number Problem last Friday, "inspiring" me to lock myself up all weekend. In my night-time visions he had been my guide in the mountains, leading me astray. And now he was waiting for me outside my office. Like a missionary with a nose for lost souls, he was on my track, eager to convert me to his disturbed beliefs.

"I simply must speak to you, professor."

"You spoke to me on Friday afternoon. You know you're not allowed to do this." I hid my panic underneath a harsh tone of voice. The look in his eyes reminded me too much of what I had just seen in my bathroom mirror.

"I am well aware of committing a transgression, professor. Which should be an indication to you that I have come on a matter of considerable urgency."

Crowding me as I unlocked the door to my office, he followed me inside.

I sat down in my office chair and wheeled it over to the filing cabinet. Opening the top drawer, I began searching through my papers. Mr. Vale was now standing behind me, looking over my shoulder.

"As you will recall, last Friday we discussed the Wild Number Problem."

This could not be happening! I swung around to face him. "Mr. Vale, would you please be so kind as to leave my office? Can't you see I'm busy?"

"Yes, professor, I can see," he acknowledged with a tender smile, "And may you stay busy for many years to come. Let that be the very reason for this inopportune visit: I have come to warn you that you are in danger."

"What on earth are you talking about?"

"They are onto us, professor."

"Who? Who is onto us? What do you mean 'us'?"

"Because of its far-reaching consequences, all sorts of dubious interest groups are trying to obtain information about my Wild Number Theorem. You, Professor Swift, being the only person in whom I have confided with regards to my spectacular discovery, have unfortunately become their prime target. Unlikely as it may sound to you, I have strong evidence implicating two of your most cherished students. I regret having to inform you that the young lad known to you as Peter Wong is in fact Li Chu, a secret agent working for the Chinese government, while his inseparable companion Sebastian O'Grady, whose real name is Timothy Kirkpatrick, has direct ties with the Irish Republican Army and is on Scotland Yard's Most Wanted list."

"That's ridiculous." Shaking my head, I went back to searching through my files. In a way, Mr. Vale's story came as a relief. It was so clearly nonsensical that it reassured me of my own mental health. But his presence in my office still oppressed me, his runaway imagination preventing me from collecting my thoughts. He was now leaning over me. I could smell his stale breath.

"Your skepticism does not come as a complete surprise," he said. "I must confess that I too, at first refused to believe it, enchanted as I was by their sprightly intellects. Sadly, their innocent enthusiasm is but a guise, rehearsed down to the smallest detail in the training-camps of their commanders. But please, professor, let us not get carried away lamenting the loss of two young souls who have succumbed to the temptations of evil. We must remain vigilant, for even greater dangers lurk in these hallowed halls. The enemy has infiltrated the very ranks of the university staff. I must admit that it was a brilliant decoy maneuver, to be the only one to refuse me a weekly fifteen-minute audience. A stroke of genius, to qualify my work as nonsense. But I saw right through your colleague. Professor Oberdorfer is the one masterminding the campaign to steal my theory! With his unquenchable thirst for power, fame and wealth, he is willing to sell my theorem to the highest bidders, regardless of their sinister purposes."

"Come, come, Mr. Vale. What is there to be gained from wild numbers? They have no practical use whatsoever." This was the argument Kate always used against my work. "Now if you don't mind, I'd like to prepare for my class."

"Your naïveté surprises me, Professor Swift," he went on relentlessly. "Need I remind you that together with their mysterious cousins, the prime numbers, wild numbers are used in making codes? With the aid of my theorem, such codes can now be cracked with the greatest of ease. The implications are dramatic: just think, if you will, of all the painstakingly encoded confidential information in the files of insurance companies and hospitals, of banks and police stations, all of a sudden freely accessible for vindictive neighbors, muckraking journalists and other malevolent figures? But such dangers pale in comparison to the effects my theorem will have on military intelligence. Did you know, for instance, that the electronics guiding nuclear warheads, the homing devices of so-called 'smart' weapons, are encoded on the basis of wild numbers? Using my findings, the enemy can not only decode the homing device and render it harmless, he can alter the flight path at will, sending the missile straight back to the sender should he so desire. A haunting image hovers before my mind's eye, Professor Swift, of such a deadly weapon poised above New York, above Paris, London or any other Western metropolis, programmed in a macabre choreography to twirl and do loop-the-loops or whatever else might tickle the enemy's morbid fancy before he sends it plunging into the horror-stricken multitudes."

"And what do you suggest we do about it?" I said, closing the top drawer of the filing cabinet and opening the middle one.

"Do I perchance detect a note of flippancy in your voice, professor? I do not blame you. Indeed, the implications of my theory at first seemed like science fiction to me too, but then, who would have thought the destruction of Hiroshima and Nagasaki lay concealed within Albert Einstein's simple formula $e=mc^2$? I beseech you, professor, for the sake of humanity, for the sake of our planet, to keep away from the people I mentioned earlier and to lie low, yes, perhaps even to go into hiding for as long as it takes."

It was one minute to nine. I slammed the middle drawer shut and opened the bottom one. "And how long might that be?"

"Until I have worked out the complex logistics needed to snatch my theorem from the jaws of doom. For it is of paramount importance that it be made public everywhere all at once, not only in mathematical periodicals, but in newspapers and in radio and television broadcasts all over the world. Messengers will even have to be dispatched to isolated settlements deep in the rainforest, to the tent camps of desert nomads and to shepherd's huts in remote mountain valleys. That is the only way to prevent one party from having an unfair advantage over the rest. Glorious times may yet lie ahead, professor, for if my theorem is accessible to mankind as a whole, hoarding information will become an impossibility. Knowledge and technology will be shared by all, the guarding of secrets will be considered a pitiful obsession of past generations. It is not in my nature to boast, Professor Swift, but do not be surprised if some day the jury report of the Swedish Academy of Science runs as follows: 'This year's Nobel Prize for Peace has been awarded to the mathematician Leonard Vale, whose Wild Number Theorem has rendered all codes ineffective, thus paving the road to worldwide dialogue and mutual trust.'"

"A glorious prospect indeed. Now if you don't mind, I must get to my class."

I gathered my books and headed for the door. With a jolt that made my jaws clamp shut, I was stopped dead in my tracks and found myself looking straight into Mr. Vale's eyes: his hand was planted firmly on my chest.

"We must not be seen leaving this office together," he instructed me. "I suggest you give me a two-minute head start."

Dazed, I stayed behind in my office. When I realized that by standing there I was giving him exactly the head start he had asked for, I was quick to move. Still shaky from the confrontation, I mounted the stairs to room 207, where my students were noisily awaiting my arrival.

The moment I walked in, they flocked around me like bleating sheep.

"Sir, do we have to know Chapter 3..." "Mr. Swift, could you explain how..." "How come quaternions and octonions are the only..."

Gesticulating wildly I summoned everyone to sit down.

Mr. Vale meanwhile had chosen his favorite seat in the front row and was busy setting up his tape recorder.

"Good morning, professor," he said cheerfully.

With a click, the two reels of his monstrous machine began to turn. I was overcome with a primitive fear that my soul was being sucked in, enabling Mr. Vale to exercise his diabolical powers over me whenever and wherever he pleased. I cleared my throat and hurriedly began enumerating the chapters that my students had to know for the exam. Then I moved to the board to write something down. My hand trembled when I pressed the chalk against the board. It broke in two, and as I bent down to pick up the piece that had broken off, I hit my elbow against the aluminum ledge attached to the bottom of the blackboard. Pull yourself together, Isaac Swift! I said to myself. Chalk has a tendency to break, elbows tend to bump into things. Chances were that the students had not noticed anything unusual about me.

"As you can see," I said to the flock that was gaping dumbly at my every move, "in order to prove that the group *K* is commutative, we must first define the element of unity." I was pleasantly surprised by my calm tone of voice.

"But sir," one of the students whined. "How come *K* is commutative?"

"Hey, what a coincidence," I joked. "That's what I was wondering too."

The others laughed heartily, and I exploited the moment to gain more confidence, treating the poor student to the notorious mathematician's smirk. But when the laughter in the room persisted, in a flash of panic I checked whether my fly was open, then concealed this anxiety by wiping the chalk dust from the elbow of my jacket.

"Now $e*a$ equals $a*e$ equals e, therefore e equals a," I said, writing the line down on the board. "It follows that a equals its own reciprocal, hence $a*b^{-1}$ is an element of the group." Once again, I was amazed to hear myself making so much sense. Everything seemed to be in order, as long as I avoided looking at Mr. Vale. This was not easy: given his prominent position in the front row, my gaze kept being drawn to the slowly revolving reels of his tape recorder. They made me go cross-eyed and distorted my sense of balance. In search of support I leaned against the blackboard, forgetting that it was made up of two movable panels. I felt myself falling and stepped back just in time. The students were watching me with big, attentive eyes. Evidently, my strange behavior still had not fallen within the visible spectrum. I wrote down the remaining steps of the proof. "And so," I concluded with relief, "$e*a$ equals $a*e$ equals e, therefore..." I stopped in mid-sentence. The exact same line was already written on the board. Somehow, I had gone around in a circle.

I stared long and hard at my proof, but could not find the place where I had gone wrong. Behind my back, the students had begun to stir.

"Mr. Swift, I think you skipped a step." It was Peter Wong's voice.

Turning to face the class, I saw that Mr. Vale's eyes had grown wide with fear. Li Chu, the Chinese spy!

"You haven't properly defined the element of unity," Peter explained.

"Where?" I was totally lost. "Here?"

"No no no, not that e, the other one!" cried Sebastian O'Grady, alias Timothy Kirkpatrick.

"This one?"

"Yes!"

"That's the element of unity."

Peter's lips slowly curled to form a smirk.

"I don't see the problem," I had to confess.

"You can't just claim that those two elements are commutative without first showing that the reciprocal of *b* is an element of the group. Otherwise *e* cannot possibly be the element of unity, at least not as long as there is a possibility that the two elements are not commutative."

"Isn't that what I just did over there?" I inquired meekly. Distracted by Mr. Vale's grimaces, no doubt intended as warning signals, I had not followed a word of Peter's explanation.

The smirk persisted. "That is exactly what you didn't do over there."

The rest of the class sniggered. The bleating sheep had turned into bloodthirsty wolves.

I didn't know what to do. When it comes to making mistakes, mathematicians are merciless. What would my students care that I had only three hours of sleep or that Mr. Vale had just about assaulted me in my own office? A mistake was a mistake. My only instinct was to flee.

"May I?" Peter Wong said, nodding at the board and already rising from his seat.

It was painful to see with how much flair he chalked down the proof, explaining every step with great precision and answering his fellow students' queries as if he had been teaching all his life. When he was through, the class rewarded him with a big round of applause.

"Here you go sir," he said, offering me his piece of chalk.

From everywhere in the room, smirking faces were observing me.

"Sir?"

"Carry on, Peter," I muttered, and walked straight out of the classroom.

An hour later, I was pacing through my living room wondering what had come over me. In a fit of panic I had walked out on my students, proving for all to see that I had lost control over myself. And it was the very last class of the year: the image of my ignoble exit would linger in their minds all summer. I considered calling every last one of them to apologize for my unprofessional behavior, spending hours on the phone answering all their questions, organizing a marathon class the next day and letting everybody pass the exam with flying colors. "You stupid prick!" I said. "You fucking moron!" When the living room became too small to contain my self-reproach, I lengthened my route to include the other rooms of my apartment, all rooms, that is, except my study, which housed the source of all my troubles. "You're talking out loud, you idiot. Shut up!" I wondered whether I was on my way to becoming one of those disturbed people that I sometimes encountered on the street, who conversed with mailboxes and swore at garbage cans. "Shut the fuck up and sit down!" But I was too high-strung to stay on the sofa for long, soon bouncing up and resuming my troubled pacing. When the phone rang, I froze. It could very well be the dean of our faculty summoning me to his office to persuade me to do the honorable thing and submit my resignation. My hand remained poised just above the receiver. "All right, Isaac. Answer the phone. Just answer the goddamn phone."

"Hello?"

"Good morning once again, professor, this is Leonard Vale speaking."

"Mr. Vale..." I began sternly.

"Please, please," he interrupted me. "I know you are a busy man, and I do not wish to detain you from your work. I would just like to congratulate you for your brilliant performance this morning in class. Li Chu and his contemptible henchman Timothy Kirkpatrick were on the verge of making a move, but thanks to your brilliant ploy, your masterful show of confusion, you drew them into the spotlight, forcing them to help out with that innocuous mathematical problem so as not to blow their cover. You pinned Li Chu against the blackboard, professor, as it were. It was a delightful spectacle. I had thought it impossible, Professor Swift, but my esteem for you has risen yet again."

"Thank you, Mr. Vale," I sighed. "Thank you for calling."

"You are the one to be thanked, professor," he said, and hung up.

"Crazy son-of-a-bitch," I laughed into the receiver before putting it down.

My gratitude had been quite sincere, for once again, his nonsense reassured me that my critical faculties were in order. It was time to see things in proper perspective. True, I had made a fool of myself in class. Brought about by a combination of fatigue and Mr. Vale's distressing visit to my office, I had made a mistake of an embarrassingly elementary nature and had been unable to recognize it as such even when Peter pointed it out to me. Retracing the steps of the proof in peace and quiet, I now saw with crystalline clarity where I had gone wrong. No, with more than that; for no crystal, however pure, could ever be as clear as mathematical truth. Walking out of a class was inexcusable, but not the end of the world; as long as I could distinguish right from wrong. Five plus three did not equal nine. It never had and it never would. As long as I let the truth and nothing but the truth be my guide, Mr. Vale's disturbed mind could never lead me astray.

I entered my study and sat down at my desk. As a new surge of inspiration and determination carried me deeper into the realm of wild numbers, the morning down at the university faded into the background, seeming like little more now than a bad dream.

7

Assuming there is a set of pseudo-wild prime numbers Q_p that is infinite and K-reducible, find a correspondence between the elements q_p and w_p—wild primes—such that for every pseudo-wild prime there exists at least one wild prime…

"What do you mean, assume Q_p is infinite and K-reducible? You are only shifting the problem!"

"What's wrong with shifting the problem? Isn't that how Heinrich Riedel found his theorem?"

"Yes, but you're no Heinrich Riedel."

"Oh yeah? And who the hell are you?"

"I'm Isaac Swift."

"So am I."

"Stop it, both of you!" I said. "I'm trying to get some work done here."

"Well, well, well: a third voice! Join the party!"

"One little two little three little Isaacs," I sang, "Four little five little six little Isaacs…"

I switched to a falsetto to imitate Kate's voice. "This is the pathological state known as dissociation. The patient's mind breaks up into numerous complexes, each of which functions more or less autonomously…"

"And how long have you been suffering from this affliction?"

"Well doctor, it all began with a mathematical problem known as the Wild Number Problem."

"You and I, Professor Swift, are in grave danger."

"Shut up, all of you! I am trying to concentrate!"

The key was to find two suitable sub-sets of T and W, proving at least one wild number corresponded to every tame number, then proving the tame sub-set contained an infinite number of elements. I had already set up correspondences for several trivial finite sub-sets. But the larger the set, the more difficult it was to establish a clearly definable correspondence between tame and wild elements. If only I could find one of Dimitri's so-called calibrator sets. That would do the trick.

"Carry on, Peter," I muttered, interrupting my reflection. Blood rushed to my cheeks when I thought of how I had walked out on my students. It was now a week ago, a week in which I had locked myself up in my apartment and had spoken to no one. My habit of speaking out loud was out of control: every move, whether it was physical or mental, prompted an immediate response from a hoard of commentators.

"Carry on, Peter," I said again.

"Your element of unity is under-defined," he observed.

How appropriate, I thought, for someone who was falling apart to have under-defined his element of unity!

The only way to stop the voices was to concentrate on the Wild Number Problem. But no matter how far I ventured into that obscure realm, I did not seem to come any closer to a solution. Quite the contrary: I was like somebody who, having lost his bearings, instead of staying put and collecting his thoughts, foolishly sets out towards a point in the distance vaguely resembling a familiar landmark, only to realize upon arriving there that wishful thinking has been his only guide. Whenever I arrived at such a false landmark, the commentators who had temporarily vanished would zero in on me with redoubled ferocity.

"*You* are trying to solve the Wild Number Problem?" I asked myself, adopting Larry's arrogant tone of voice.

"And what's wrong with that?"

"Oh, nothing. Nothing at all. By all means carry on." But at the same time, I curled my lips into one of his devastating smirks.

Was I possessed? It certainly seemed that way. I could feel what it was like to be Larry, his intense scorn coming from somewhere deep within me. Dimitri was there as well, though not as a voice. When I imagined how he would react to my wild number investigations, my eyes became doleful and I shook my wise head at so much foolishness.

"In a weak personality like Isaac's," Kate lectured, "there are not enough defenses to prevent friends and acquaintances from being internalized, where destructive instincts act upon them like a leavening agent, turning them into potent demonic forces. I myself am a prime example of such a force."

"Thanks for your commentary, darling."

"My pleasure, sweetheart."

Nights were the worst. Kate had once told me that lack of sleep and an improper diet could trigger a psychosis. This worried me. A week of instant soup and dry bread could hardly be considered healthy, and in the past nights I had not slept for more than an hour at a time, kept awake by confused reflections on the Wild Number Problem interspersed with angry voices, bizarre fantasies and the annoying nonsense rhyme that I had thought up for the wedding of my friends:

> Anne and Stan, Stan and Anne
> from the jungles of the Yucatan
> to the mountains of Afghanistan.

"That's pathetic," Betty Lane commented from behind the tropical fern.

"I'd switch to artificial intelligence if I were you," I said with the booming voice of Vernon Ludlow, the gastroenterologist. "You would be doing something useful for a change."

"Amen!" Kate agreed. Her voice seemed to come from the extra pillow in my bed.

Rolling onto my other side, I turned into the youthful Anatole Millechamps de Beauregard, the Mozart among mathematicians and the life of every party, reciting a brilliant ballad in honor of his friends. While Larry Oberdorfer and Vernon Ludlow, in early nineteenth-century garb, stood in the shadows eyeing me jealously, a flock of admiring ladies with powdered faces had gathered around me, their breasts bulging enticingly out of their tight bodices.

"Aha!" Kate cried. "Aha! Your true motives are coming to the surface at last."

"Shut up for a minute," I said, shoving the possessed pillow out of bed.

The trick was to construct a series of infinite sets of pseudo-wild numbers such that their intersection contained wild numbers only. But either the definition for pseudo-wildness was too weak, so that the set contained tame numbers as well, or it was too strong, so that the set remained empty. A calibrator set. A calibrator set. If only I found a suitable calibrator set!

"It's hopeless," I sighed.

"But there is no need to solve the Wild Number Problem, professor. I have already done so."

"Anne and Stan, Stan and Anne..."

I threw the blankets away and got out of bed.

My insomnia called for drastic measures. In the kitchen, I took a fork out of the drawer, pressed its prongs against the inside of my wrist, and dragged it down the length of my forearm. It left a trail of four parallel white lines, which slowly faded and then returned brighter than before, gradually turning pink. Here and there, droplets of blood appeared. The pain felt pleasant, like a mild sunburn, and by studying the lines I managed to keep the voices at bay.

Parallel sets of wild numbers? Was that the solution? But what did I mean by parallel sets?

Once, when I was eight years old, I took one of the silver forks that my mother reserved for special occasions and was so engrossed in scratching a grid pattern on my belly that I did not notice her coming into the kitchen. "Isaac!" she cried, snatching the fork from me and slapping me on the hand. "Have you gone out of your mind?" As punishment she had me polish all the silverware. At first I wept bitterly, but the burning sensation spreading over my belly and the gleaming silver soon made me forget my mother's anger. I became fascinated by my reflection in one of the spoons that I had just polished, first studying the concave side which produced an upside-down image, then the convex side which made my eyes bulge more and more as I moved the spoon closer to my face. "He is such a strange boy," I overheard my mother saying to her friend Alice on the phone. "Do you think I should have someone look at him?" It became a ritual that lasted into adolescence: whenever I was feeling unhappy I would seek solace by scratching patterns on my skin with a fork.

Parallel sets. I didn't quite know what I meant, but it was worth looking into.

"Such a strange boy," I muttered, getting up from the kitchen table and going to my study for yet another attempt to crack the Wild Number Problem.

A series of so-called parallel sub-sets with no common elements, each tracing a unique path of wild numbers...

It was difficult to concentrate. The heat emanating from the scratches in my arm was making me drowsy.

"Very good, professor! That is what I have been trying to tell you all along. There is no need to concentrate. The work has been done. Allow me to suggest you get some sleep now. We have a long day ahead of us."

Mr. Vale and I were high up in the mountains, warming ourselves by a campfire in the early dawn. We were fleeing from Larry Oberdorfer and his henchmen Li Chu and Timothy Kirkpatrick and had to reach the pass by noon, or they would overtake us and steal Mr. Vale's findings, with which they could destroy the world. Beyond the pass lay the Land of Vale, where five plus three equalled nine and everybody was happy all the time.

"Sleep, professor, sleep tight. I shall watch over you."

When I next opened my eyes, I was swimming in a rough sea, monstrous waves white with foam about to crash down on me. But the waves were merely the upturned corners of the papers lying on my desk. Lifting my head, I became aware of the ringing telephone. I wiped away the trail of spittle that ran from the corner of my mouth and hurried to the living-room.

It was Dimitri. "It's been so long since I've seen you. I was wondering whether you were ill."

"No, not at all." I was dazed by the bright sunlight in the room and by the fact that I was having a conversation with a real human being for the first time in a week. "I've been working at home the last couple of days."

"I see."

Was it my imagination or did he sound skeptical?

"Speaking of your work, I would enjoy hearing how it has been coming along lately. If you can find the time to drop by..."

"Sure. Of course. That would be nice." In my efforts to sound normal I was overdoing my cheerfulness.

"How about right now? I have spent the whole day marking exams. I could certainly use an elevating conversation with a colleague."

"The whole day?" Puzzled, I looked at the clock on the kitchen wall. Sure enough, it was past four o'clock in the afternoon.

"Well, I didn't have much else to do, and with this fine weather I felt sorry for the teaching assistants, so I thought I'd help them out. So Isaac, how about it?"

"How about what? Oh. Yes, sure. I'll be right down."

When I had hung up, a sense of doom fell like a blanket upon my shoulders. How could I face Dimitri? He wanted to discuss my research. What research? I had done absolutely nothing with the material he had given me, other than misuse it for my foolish attacks on the Wild Number Problem. And then there was that walkout incident. He would certainly demand an explanation. Inviting me down to the university was just a pretext to discuss my mental health. Hadn't he asked me if I was ill? One fatherly hand on my shoulder and I would break down completely. I pictured him larger than life, his warmth and wisdom engulfing me as he lifted me up and cradled me to sleep like a baby.

"Grow up, Swift," I growled. In the bathroom, I did my best to make myself look presentable. After shaving off my week-old beard, I rummaged through the medicine cabinet and found an old bottle of eyedrops. I ignored the expiration date and emptied the contents into my bloodshot eyes. The excess fluid ran down my cheeks, making it look as if I were crying. "Forgive me, Dimitri," I recited, my voice wavering melodramatically. "Forgive me my sins." Hurriedly I splashed cold water over my face and went to get dressed, choosing a long-sleeved shirt to conceal the four dotted lines of scab on my arm.

Dimitri was poring over an enormous atlas when I entered his office. It was opened to a page showing the area between Moscow and the northern shores of the Caspian Sea.

"Isn't this beautiful?" he said. "There was a dump sale of these in the Campus Book Store. With the boundaries in Eastern Europe and the former Soviet Union changing so fast, they aren't much use anymore to students of political science. Just think of those poor cartographers nowadays, working day and night to keep up with the most recent developments, almost like journalists."

I made an effort to laugh. It was nice of him to engage me in friendly conversation before bringing down the hammer, but I would have preferred to get it done and over with immediately.

"When I was a child, I often dreamed of sailing down the Volga to the Caspian Sea," he said, tracing the course of the river with his finger. "My little state-sponsored excursion to Volgograd was as far as I ever got. Maybe one day when I am too old for mathematics... although the real thing could very well turn out to be a disappointment."

"Yes, you could be right." Yes Dimitri, as you say, Dimitri, please, Dimitri, hurry up and shoot me.

"I have always been intrigued by the colors that cartographers use to indicate altitude, especially by the dark green for areas below sea-level," he mused, gently stroking the area around the Caspian Sea. "I suppose the colors were chosen to suggest the terrain that we associate with the various altitudes: greens for the grasslands and forests of the lowlands, browns for the rock masses and barren plateaus of the highlands, purple and white for the snowy mountain peaks. But sometimes they are misleading. Take this dark green area around the Caspian Sea. In reality it is quite barren, certainly as you move south towards Iran. Or take Death Valley."

Oblivious of my growing impatience, he leafed at leisure through the atlas until he found the page showing southern California. He pointed to a long gash of dark green in an expansive region of various browns. "The way it is depicted here, you might think of a lush valley in the middle of the desert. Yet it is one of the most desolate places I have ever had the pleasure of visiting. Oh well. I guess this sort of deception is the price we must pay for trying to express two things at once."

"I'm sorry, but could you please get to the point?"

"I beg your pardon?" As a respected scholar, Dimitri was accustomed to being listened to. Rudeness was such a rare phenomenon in his universe that my outburst bewildered rather than offended him.

"You didn't invite me down here just to admire your atlas. You want to know why I haven't come up with any results this past year. You want to know why I walked out on my class the other day. I know. Don't tell me. It was unpardonable to leave them like that, especially just before the exam, and..."

He raised his hand to stop my cascade of self-reproach. "Please. I wouldn't worry too much on that last score. Peter told me that he and Sebastian took turns answering the other students' questions after you had left. And judging by the exams I marked today, they did a fine job finishing up the excellent job you have done all year. Only five students failed! But still, it is a bit strange that you just walked out. So, to be honest: you are right, I did not invite you down here to look at maps. I would like to know what is troubling you."

"I'm not sure," I said glumly. Tempting though it was to spill out all my woes, any mention of the wild numbers was out of the question. With such a brilliant scholar sitting opposite me, I realized how utterly foolish my struggles of the past two weeks had been.

"You look tired. Could it be that you are working too hard?"

"Evidently I am not nearly working hard enough!" I said with a bitter laugh. As I spoke, I kept my eyes focused on the green gash in the map of California, fearing that Dimitri's mild expression would reduce me to tears. "Since my thesis I have achieved absolutely nothing worthwhile. The way things are going I might not be able to hold onto this job for very much longer."

"You cannot force results. You will only end up hating what you are doing. Results, publications, job security: only too often, such concerns are death to inspiration."

"That is easy for you to say," I blurted out. My childishly resentful tone of voice disgusted me, but I was unable to contain myself. "You can look back on a successful career. When you were my age, you were already an internationally renowned mathematician."

Dimitri waved away my words. "It so happens that when I was your age, I was going through one of the most difficult periods in my career."

"Oh? Really?"

"You don't believe me, do you? But it's true. Grossly over-estimating my mathematical powers, I had led myself to believe that I was on the verge of solving the Wild Number Problem."

"The Wild Number Problem?" I asked guardedly.

"Yes. When I had proved there was a relationship between wild numbers and prime numbers, I did not publish my proof immediately, thinking that I was just steps away from a far more spectacular discovery. Once it turned out I was wrong, I had terrible trouble persuading myself to publish the lesser result. In retrospect a beautiful theorem, of course, but at the time not nearly as beautiful as I had hoped, leaving me bitterly disappointed."

"You can't be serious. That was the first major breakthrough in over half a century."

"But I am. Partial success can be more frustrating than no success at all. Haven't you ever seen silver medalists weeping on the victory stand? In fact, I was so disillusioned that I lost all interest in mathematics. Sometimes I think that it was this disappointment more than idealism that made me shift my attention to politics. An unfortunate decision, as you know."

I left a respectful silence while he returned to the page in the atlas showing where it had all taken place. Dimitri rarely spoke of this painful episode in his life. In response to his politically charged welcoming speech at a mathematics conference in Moscow, the authorities stripped him of his position at the university and sent him to a psychiatric institute in Volgograd to be cured of his anti-communist delusions. After eleven months of confinement among the criminally insane, he was released thanks to mounting pressure from the international mathematical community, his sentence being converted to life-long exile from the Soviet Union. It took five more years of pulling strings before his wife and two daughters were allowed to join him.

"It was here," he said, pointing to the red spot just north of the Caspian Sea, "locked up among those poor deranged souls, that I found back my love for mathematics. I should be grateful to the authorities for granting me the opportunity to get to the bare essence of my passion. In that human zoo, my failure to solve the Wild Number Problem no longer mattered to me, nor did my successes in other areas. All that mattered was the intense well-being that I felt whenever I was engaged in mathematical thought. Mathematics was like water to me, the only clear and refreshing substance amid the filth, indeed, the only substance without a smell. For my God, Isaac, the stench in that place was indescribable!" He rubbed his nose, as if the foul odors had to be dispelled once again. "Because of the drugs they gave me, my mind was too clouded to come up with anything new, and I was unable to concentrate for longer than five minutes at a time, but even those tiny sips of mathematics were lovely, and more than enough to maintain my sanity." Dimitri fell silent. Staring at the guilty spot on the map, he withdrew into an endlessly deep, untouchable part of his soul. I did not dare to disturb him.

"You have put me to shame, Dimitri," I said at last. "My problems seem so trivial beside what you went through."

"But that was not my intention," he said, smiling cheerfully as he closed the atlas. "What I wanted to say before I got carried away by my life story was that it sometimes helps to take distance from your work. Luckily there are more enjoyable ways to do this than by letting yourself be locked up in a psychiatric institution."

"Such as...?" I asked, eager to drop the topic of psychiatry.

"Well, it is only a suggestion, but why don't you go on leave for a while? I am willing to wager that half a year from now you'll come running back, thirsting for mathematics!"

"So you are sending me away."

"Isaac! You know better than that."

Yes, of course I knew better, but that didn't take away the feeling of being rejected. I stared at the edge of the desk, fighting back my tears.

"I'm afraid I have got to be on my way now," he said. "We are taking our grandchildren to the puppet theater this evening. But before you go, I would like you to accept this as a gift." He slid the atlas across the table.

"What for?" Annoyed by his absurd generosity, I tried to push the atlas back to him.

"Go on, take it," he said. "I can always buy another one. It might inspire you to consider my suggestion instead of merely being offended by it. There are so many wonderful places to see in this world."

That evening, I sat on the sofa with the atlas on my lap, absently leafing through it while the voices swarmed around me.

"The Great Dimitri Arkanov has spoken. You have been exiled from his palace."

"Well well well, a leave of absence! The world is going to pieces and his lordship is off to solve his personal problems. Oh the poor boy, poor little Isaac."

"You should be ashamed of yourself, carrying on like a child in front of such an eminent scholar. I'm surprised he didn't invite you along to the puppet theater!"

Reviewing the conversation in Dimitri's office, I concluded that I was a lesser human being in every respect. An obscene clown. Working on the Wild Number Problem indeed! If Dimitri, of all people, claimed that he had over-estimated himself when studying the problem, how could I possibly justify my half-baked efforts?

Yet underneath the shame, there was a dawning sense of relief. With those wild numbers I had been headed straight towards disaster. My visit to Dimitri's office had come just in time; he had plucked me out of the chaos and set me down on my feet.

I tried to imagine what it would mean, no mathematics for half a year. How would I fill the void? I had no hobbies to speak of, no social life to attend to. Grudgingly, I admitted that Kate may have been right after all, that I had neglected the largest part of my personality, and that it was high time–I had to swallow to fight the bad taste in my mouth–"to listen to my emotions." Perhaps, as Dimitri had suggested, a trip to some exotic destination would be a good way to "find myself," or whatever it was that travellers were supposed to do. I now looked through the atlas with greater interest. Studying the map of China, I was drawn to a dark green spot north of Tibet called the Tu fan Depression. I remembered Dimitri's observation about the coloring of maps, and wondered what the place really looked like. I searched through the atlas for other areas below sea level: the region around the Caspian Sea, Lake Eyre in Australia, the polders of the Netherlands, the Qattara Depression in Egypt. I stopped at the green gash in southern California. Knowing from school that Death Valley was one of the hottest places on earth, I pictured myself standing on the valley floor, two hundred eighty-two feet below sea-level, looking across dazzling white saltflats at the yellow sand dunes in the distance, trembling in the heat. White and yellow, not dark green: in Dimitri's words, the price we had to pay for trying to express two things at once. And then I saw the solution.

I left the atlas on the sofa and went to my study. In a state of complete calm and deep concentration, step by step without the slightest hesitation, I wrote down the solution to the Wild Number Problem. I cannot possibly reconstruct how a depression in southern California provided the key. All I know is that it did, once again proving the cliché that the best way to find something is to give up looking for it.

"I can't believe it," I said, when I had completed the three-page proof. Sure enough–as generations of mathematicians had tried in vain to show–there were an infinite number of wild numbers. "Unbelievable."

And then a strange thing happened. Instead of rejoicing, I panicked.

After too many nights of pushing my intellect beyond its limits, of banging my head against solid rock in a desperate attempt to make it budge, taunted by inner voices telling me what a despicable being I was, I did not dare to believe that I could simply climb to the solution without encountering any resistance. It was a trap. It had to be. I went over the steps of my proof again, and again and again, without finding the error I hoped for. At the same time, another part of me had rushed ahead: it stood on the mountain pass, catching its breath as it watched the sun rising over a land that no human eyes had ever yet beheld, lighting up valley after valley in wondrous color. But there had to be a mistake somewhere. How could I, Isaac Swift, have solved the Wild Number Problem?

"It can't be right. It can't be right," I sobbed, beating the desktop with my fist. "It can't be right."

"Welcome, professor," said a voice, "Welcome to the Land of Vale."

8

"Yeah?" said Stan with a dull voice.

"Hello Stan, it's me, Isaac."

"What the hell? It's two o'clock in the morning!"

"I'm sorry, I didn't know who else to call."

"It's Isaac," Stan whispered to Anne, who I heard grumbling in the background. Then he addressed me again: "What's wrong? Are you sick or something?"

"I'm not sure. Well, yes, I guess so. I think I've gone insane."

"What are you talking about? You haven't been taking drugs, have you?"

"No no, that isn't it. No."

"Then what the hell's the matter with you?"

"I can't explain over the phone. Please, could you come over?"

"You've got to be kidding."

I left a silence.

"All right. I'll be right over. Don't do anything strange in the mean time, okay?"

Twenty minutes later he was at my door. Even at this hour he exuded health and happiness. "Good morning Isaac," he said cheerily, patting me on the shoulder as he made his way towards the living room. He sat down on the sofa, carefully moving the opened atlas that was still lying there to the side. "How about coffee for starters?"

"Sorry, I've run out. Shall I make tea? Or no, I'm out of that too."

"Never mind. I'll settle for water."

When I returned from the kitchen with two glasses of water, Stan was looking at a page in the atlas showing the Yucatan Peninsula, where he and Anne were going on their honeymoon.

"Well now," he said with a dry smile. "You were saying you had gone insane."

Good old Stan. How wrong I had been lately, to discard him as dull and complacent. He was one of those refreshing people who made the world seem endlessly less complicated just by walking into a room.

"Well, to begin with, I have been hearing voices." I had to convince myself again that there really was a problem.

"What kind of voices?"

I told him how I was having whole arguments with myself out loud.

"Look, I'm not an expert. Since my internships I haven't done any psychiatry. But have these voices been telling you to do things you normally wouldn't do?"

"No, not really," I was forced to admit after thinking it over.

Stan was unimpressed. "Everybody talks out loud once in a while. Especially when you've been alone for a long time. I remember the crazy conversations I had with myself as an intern on night-call."

"That isn't all," I said, rolling up my sleeve. "Look!"

"Gee, an arm."

"No, here!" I pointed at the scratches, which had all but disappeared. "I did this with a fork last night."

"Mm," Stan frowned, "That is a bit weird. Not that you chose a very effective method, but you haven't been contemplating suicide, have you?

"No. I was hoping that the pain would help take my mind off mathematics."

"A bit kinky, but it does makes sense. How have you been sleeping lately?"

"Two hours a night, three hours at most. But yesterday I fell asleep at my desk and woke up at four o'clock this afternoon."

"Okay. My diagnosis is that you have been working too hard and not getting enough sleep. Other than that, you seem perfectly normal, or at least not more abnormal than usual." He reached into his pocket and placed a bottle of pills on the table. "Take one or two of these every night. You'll sleep wonderfully. Anne sometimes takes them too."

"No Stan, wait. You don't understand. I was able to explain away all these symptoms just like you, that is, until what happened tonight."

I told him the whole story of the wild numbers.

Stan shook his head. "You don't need a doctor. You should consult a mathematician."

"If only that were true. This has nothing to do with mathematics. It's purely psychological. My critical faculties have failed me completely. The solution just can't be right."

"Why not? Or is that a stupid question?"

"It can't be right. It just can't be."

"Sure, Isaac, just like it couldn't be right that you graduated with honors, just like it was a grave mistake that you were offered a job even before finishing your Ph.D. thesis, it being the worst in the history of mankind. I gave up trusting your gloomy predictions long ago. You were going to die as a virgin, remember?"

"This is different," I said, suppressing a smile. "It's too spectacular. It would be like you finding the cure to cancer or malaria. Well, maybe not that spectacular, but close enough."

"So? All the better for you. Listen. Why don't you get a good night's sleep and look at your proof afresh tomorrow morning? Maybe then you'll spot the mistake, assuming there is one. Or better yet, leave it lying around for a week."

"I cannot stand that prospect, Stan. Every minute that my so-called theorem lives on is sheer torture."

"Then have a colleague look at it. How about that Russian genius you keep telling me about?"

"Dimitri? No. I couldn't. I would be too ashamed."

"Somebody else, then?"

My heart sank. "There is only one other person who knows enough about this subject. Larry Oberdorfer. Oh well, he looks down on me anyway, so I suppose it wouldn't hurt."

"There you go again!" Stan laughed. "Suppose, just for the sake of argument, that your theorem really is correct. Or is such bliss too much to bear for a pessimist like you?"

I shrugged my shoulders.

"Good. Then who would you rather show your marvelous discovery: Dimitri, whom you like, respect and trust, or Larry Oberdorfer, whom you have trouble getting along with, by the sounds of it?"

"You make it seem so easy," I sighed.

"You know Isaac, the problem with you has always been that you don't recognize good fortune even when it's staring you in the face. You have very probably just proved an important theorem. Instead of calling me in the middle of the night to come and celebrate with champagne, you scare me half to death with this bullshit about going insane."

"I'm sorry, Stan."

"Oh well. It's a change from the usual triple bypass."

Like so often in the past, Stan had brought my problems down to manageable proportions. I showed him to the door, lavishing him with words of thanks.

"Okay, I got the picture," he said. "Now before I forget: next week on Friday we're having a few people over for a barbecue. Anne asked me to invite you, provided you weren't frothing at the mouth."

"I can't guarantee that," I laughed. "You never know what might happen in the meantime."

"The fresh air will do you good. And I can let you in on a secret: we're getting the meat for next to nothing from a grateful patient, who normally delivers to restaurants only."

It is now eight days ago that I rode down to the university with knocking knees, having decided to show my proof to Dimitri.

In the office beside mine, Angela was going over the exam results with an assistant. Only too happy to delay my visit to Dimitri, I asked her how the students had done this year.

"Not bad," she said.

Peter Wong 100%, as could be expected. Sebastian O'Grady a close second, with 97%. Dave Graham, sadly, 46%. When I had run out of names and was turning to go, Angela asked me a small favor. Next week on Friday afternoon her daughter Sarah was playing Titania in the school production of *A Midsummer Night's Dream.* Could I possibly take over her fifteen minutes with Mr. Vale?

"Well, okay." He was the last person I wanted to be reminded of. I was nervous enough as it was.

"I wanted to ask Dimitri," she said apologetically. "It's just that everybody always wants his help, and the poor man is too nice to say no."

As I walked down the corridor, I thought about Angela's last remark. It was only too true, and here I was, about to burden the poor man with more work. Should I risk Larry's scorn instead? But when I stopped at his door I heard a woman giggling inside. I took a deep breath and continued to the end of the corridor. For a brief moment I hoped Dimitri wasn't in. In vain, of course. Nothing short of a nuclear disaster would keep him from the campus.

It must have seemed strange to him. Only the previous day, he had advised me to go on leave, on the assumption that I had run out of ideas. Now all of a sudden I showed up with a result. By way of introduction I told him that overnight things had gone from bad to worse, that I could no longer distinguish right from wrong and now believed I had proved the impossible.

"Let's have a look then, shall we?" Dimitri said, as if he were a doctor about to examine a patient. I handed him the proof. He removed the paper clip and spread the pages out on his desk.

"'Theorem: the set of wild numbers is infinite,'" he read the first line out loud. "My God, Isaac, why didn't you tell me you were working on this?"

"I'm sorry. I was too embarrassed. I have been dabbling in something way over my head. And now it has got out of hand."

Shaking his head, Dimitri began to study my proof. Instead of going from top to bottom, his gaze wandered in apparent aimlessness over the pages. An outsider could easily mistake this for careless and superficial reading, but what was taking place was a mark of his genius, his ability to grasp a whole system of ideas all at once.

"How strange," he said, getting up and walking to the window.

"What do you find so strange?"

Dimitri just stood there, looking across the field. Mathematicians have a habit of leaving long silences in conversations. "Ask Isaac even a simple question like 'how are you?,'" Kate once joked to our dinner guests, "and it will take him two minutes of intense thought before he feels justified to answer 'fine.'" But I had never known a silence to last a full ten minutes.

"All right, Isaac," he finally said. He sat down again and rolled up his sleeves. "We will have to go through this step by step."

"What does that mean? Do you have an idea where I went wrong?"

Without answering me, he picked up a pencil and sharpened it with great care, so that a single curl of wood fell into the wastepaper basket. Then, as he held the pencil poised above the pages, his expression became severe, as if he were an eagle soaring high above the landscape of my proof, ready to plunge down and pluck any unsuspecting error out of my reasoning.

"'Define the criterion for pseudo-wildness as follows,'" he muttered.

"I suppose my choice of terminology is debatable," I hastened to say.

"Yes, yes," Dimitri said, annoyed by the interruption. "'Clearly, the number of possible pseudo-wild sets is infinite.' Can you explain?"

Without noteworthy difficulties I proceeded to detail the reasoning implicit in the step.

"Hold it, Isaac, hold it right there. You keep using words like 'clearly' and 'obviously.' Do you think that such terms are appropriate in this context?"

"Are you saying that this step is incorrect?"

"No. I am saying that it is far more subtle than you think." On a piece of paper he showed me how easily an uninformed reader could be misled and that further specifications were needed to rule out any such confusion.

I had come to Dimitri hoping he would help my theorem out of its misery, quickly and painlessly. Yet I was relieved, and also a little bit excited, when the first few steps had passed his rigorous test with flying colors.

"I see you have used my new technique of *K*-reducibility to determine the properties of *pW*," he went on.

I gulped audibly.

"Interesting," was Dimitri's only comment. "And then, with the aid of a suitably chosen calibrator set, you analyze these so-called pseudo-wild sets, or at least, you claim that this is possible in principle." He fixed upon me his fierce eagle's eyes.

There it was, the faulty step in my reasoning. I was sure of it.

"I'm sorry, you are absolutely right. I cannot validate that claim."

"Oh, but you can. And you did, albeit rather sketchily." He showed me how I had arrived at the next step.

And so our discussion evolved along a fixed path: Dimitri would first subject the step to a brutal cross-examination, but if my defense was inadequate, he would come to the rescue by unearthing the perfectly correct reasoning that lay hidden within.

My insight of the night before was turning out to be more robust than I had dared to imagine, or was even capable of understanding. This made me wonder whether the solution to the Wild Number Problem could really be considered my discovery. Perhaps it was more accurate to say that the solution had been "out there" and had discovered me, as if it had been waiting all these years for someone in the exact right frame of mind to stumble into its territory before revealing itself. Now I was witnessing two great powers at work, Dimitri and what appeared more and more to be a genuine truth. At times I felt left out, even jealous, like someone who introduces two friends to each other who hit it off so well that he becomes superfluous. Hours passed in this manner, Dimitri frequently getting up to pace through his office, arguing passionately with the newcomer and taking less and less notice of me.

At six o'clock, there was a knock on the door. Orville, the building superintendent, came to warn us that he was locking up for the evening. When Dimitri had convinced him that we were working on what could very well turn out to be a milestone in the history of mathematics, he gave us a spare key for the side entrance. At seven, Dimitri's wife called. There was no need to know Russian to understand what the conversation was about. "Irina always thinks I work too hard," he grumbled when he had hung up. "Now where were we?" All I knew at that point was that I was sitting in the gloom. I could scarcely make out Dimitri's silhouette as he moved through the office, mumbling to himself incomprehensibly. Except for a dry biscuit with tea I hadn't eaten all day, and I squirmed in my chair to stop my stomach from grumbling. Dimitri was still as fresh as a daisy, and pursued his investigation with undiminished energy. After "we" had gone over the steps one more time, he finally switched on the light and returned to the desk, where he laid down his pencil below the bottom line of my proof.

To the end of my life I will never forget what happened next. With a strangely blank expression, Dimitri walked to the bookcase and reached for the bottle of cognac that he kept on the top shelf. When he turned to face me, there were tears in his eyes.

"Isaac, you have done it," he whispered. Pouring two generous glasses, he invited me to rise. "After so many years, I had put it out of my mind. It could just as easily have taken another century or two for the solution to be found. That I have lived to witness this glorious moment!"

We drank a toast to the birth of the Wild Number Theorem.

Dimitri took a handkerchief out of his breast pocket to wipe his eyes.

"It's so beautiful. So unbelievably beautiful. Rarely have I seen so elegant a path winding to such dizzying heights."

"Dizzying" was also the effect the alcohol was having on me. While Dimitri danced about his office, joyously throwing his arms up in the air, I felt it was wiser to sit down again.

"How did you do it, Isaac? How?"

I told him about the atlas and the areas below sea level, and how they had somehow triggered the flash of insight.

"Incredible, incredible. To think that I gave you that atlas to take your mind off mathematics!"

I asked him when exactly he had become convinced that my theorem was true.

"Right away," he said. "That was what scared me. It was too good to be true, which is why it subsequently took me all day to persuade myself that my first impression was correct. Although I must add that your gloominess of the past few months was partially to blame for my doubts as well. I wasn't prepared for anything like this."

"It took me by surprise too."

"Inspiration often does. This was clearly written in great haste, as if in a trance, with no amends made for the slower intellects among us. What you have shown me, Isaac, is the purest, most powerful example of mathematical intuition that I have come across in many, many years, perhaps in my entire life."

"Maybe I was just lucky," I said, embarrassed by so much praise. "The way the discussion went today, you would think I had no active part in finding the answer. I hardly understand what I have done."

"Don't be too humble. Intuition may be a gift from heaven, but to discern its whisper in the din of one's everyday thoughts is an art. And when you work out the details of your proof for publication, you will see that you understand more than you think you do."

"Publication?" It had been so long since I had heard the magic word.

"Of course, Isaac. You must whisk this off to *Number* as soon as possible. I'll have a word with Daniel Goldstein, the editor-in-chief. I am sure he will grant your article priority. With some luck it will be on time for the August issue. Now drink up! I'm taking you out to dinner!"

Time has flown since that glorious moment in Dimitri's office, though working out the details of my proof was not an easy task. The night that I first found the answer, I moved through the difficult terrain like a mountain goat, jumping fearlessly over dangerous gaps in our current understanding of number theory and keeping my balance on impossibly narrow ledges of reasoning. The past week I have had to retrace that tortuous path weighed down by all the mathematical tools and equipment needed for a step-by-step approach. Doubts still arose every so often, but after hours of intense concentration and an occasional phone call to Dimitri when I really got stuck, I was once again reassured. It was tough going–mathematics usually is–but instead of having to fight off nasty voices at every turn, I was now fuelled by a bubbling reservoir of joyful anticipation. Confident that the goal was within reach, I have been wise enough to stop at around ten the past few evenings and to take one or two of the sleeping pills that Stan had left me.

This morning my work was done, and I was once again in Dimitri's office to discuss the revised proof. The last remnants of my doubts evaporated in the warmth of his enthusiasm, and nothing stood in the way of sending my article to *Number*, at least, not until Mr. Vale appeared on the scene to remind me of the Friday afternoon session that I was taking over from Angela.

Only when it was too late, when he spotted my article on Dimitri's desk and began to tremble with rage, did it occur to me how his disturbed mind would put the wrong two and two together. I had plagiarized his work!

The incident in Dimitri's office was unfortunate and should have been avoided, but what did it really matter? My Wild Number Theorem was safely on its way to *Number*, and there was nothing Mr. Vale could do to stop it.

Now it was evening, a perfect summer evening to end a perfect summer day. I was drinking beer on my balcony, enjoying the view over the city. Five plus three equalled eight as never before: Dimitri had given the go-ahead and my Wild Number Theorem was on its way to *Number*, the top periodical in my field. Now all I had to do was relax and look forward to the moment that the news of my discovery would send shockwaves through the mathematical community and far beyond. In the distance, the red and white lights of the television mast flashed on and off, on and off, while indoors the phone had resumed ringing. Undoubtedly it was Mr.

Vale again. I enjoyed his unintended contribution of an acoustic variable to the already complex pattern of flashing lights. I yawned happily and swung my feet onto the railing.

Patterns. Mathematics was the love of patterns.

When I looked back at the past few weeks, it all made sense: locking myself up, staying up all night, hardly eating, even all that crazy talking out loud and scratching myself with a fork had been necessary steps leading to the deepest and farthest-reaching mathematical discovery of my life. It made sense that I had stood on the brink of going insane; to break down the barriers in my thinking had required a general breakdown. In retrospect, truth had been my guide all along, from the day in my office when Mr. Vale showed me his "solution," through the desperate weeks that followed, to the moment when I leafed through the atlas and it revealed itself to me in full splendor. But God knows how far I might have fallen if that flash of inspiration had not come to me. I shuddered at the thought.

The phone stopped ringing. Freed of its pull, I was lifted from my balcony, hovering for a moment above the treetops of the park before floating across the city towards the hypnotic flashing lights of the television mast on the horizon:

> ...red, white, red white, red white, white...
> prrrr!

– there was good old Mr. Vale again —

> red, white, red white, white red
> prrrrr!

With every ring and every flash, the pattern expanded. In the light of my solution, not only the past few weeks, but my whole life fell into a lovely geometric pattern. Powerful lines and sweeping curves from every thinkable dimension of my past converged on this single happy moment on my balcony; the long hours that I spent up in my room as a child, happily carrying ones, or descending into the realm of negative numbers, or trying to grasp the concept of infinity: these moments had paved the way to my recent discovery…

white red, white red, prrrrrr!

…but so had my mathematical hangovers, so had the lonely hours in my room where I feverishly calculated complicated formulae to blot out the happy voices of my peers playing in the streets, so had my parents' quarrels, my father's subsequent departure, my mother's undisguised favoritism for my brother Andrew: on this warm summer night, in the light of the wild numbers, the pain and sorrows of my past not only fit into the pattern, they added depth to it…

white, red prrrrrr! white red…

…and for the first time since Kate and I had gone our separate ways, there was room to remember who she really was, room to feel sadness that it had not worked out between us. We had met too early. It was that simple. My deepest passion, my love for mathematics, had not yet crystallized into success; to borrow Peter Wong's expression, my element of unity was under-defined, too under-defined for me to share my life with a woman.

The phone stopped ringing, and once again, I floated off my balcony to melt into the liquid evening. Moving my hands through the air, I traced the shapely contours of Kate's body, all my senses tingling with the memory. Now altering the pattern that I drew in the air, I conjured up the forms of an unknown woman, and altering the pattern again, of another, and another, delighting in the freedom of not yet knowing who I would fall in love with next. One thing was certain, however: now that I had solved the Wild Number Problem, I was ready for love. For contrary to what Kate had always said, contrary to my own fear that my preoccupation with mathematics was an escape, a flight into an abstract order to hide from the chaos of my emotions, I now knew for certain that love and mathematics were simply two expressions of the same passion, and that embracing the one implied embracing the other: a passion for patterns, for rhythms and form, for music and mystery, for harmony and beauty. Smiling contentedly, I reached down beside my chair for a new can of beer. A passion for life itself.

red, white, red white.

For some reason, the rhythm of the flashing lights had lost its depth, wearing too thin to carry the weight of my exalted meditations. I looked over my shoulder, wondering how long the silence inside would last. I waited patiently, but apparently Mr. Vale had finally given up hope. I tried without success to fill the gaps in the pattern by imagining the telephone had started ringing again.

Poor Mr. Vale. Now that the silence persisted, I felt a little bit guilty for having left him to his mercy. I had been so obsessed with the idea of becoming just like him, that I had forgotten he was a human being with distinct feelings of his own, disturbed feelings, perhaps, but that did not mean they could simply be brushed aside.

The silence was becoming unsettling. What was he up to? I considered looking up his sister's phone number so that I could call him back, but it was past eleven. Friendly gestures would have to wait until tomorrow. Not that I had any ideas what such a gesture might be. If he did not even see the difference between my proof and his, what would ever convince him of my innocence? Perhaps a false confession could restore a certain measure of peace in his disturbed mind. Dimitri could call us into his office to give me an official reprimand. A month later however, Mr. Vale was bound to see my article in *Number*; he was a subscriber, and whenever an issue appeared he would devote his next Friday afternoon session to refuting the entire contents. Maybe I ought to publish my article under a pseudonym. But to conceal my true identity for Mr. Vale's sake, just when success was finally coming my way: that was going overboard.

Poor Mr. Vale. The very least I could offer him tomorrow afternoon was some compassion. For the rest, all I could do was hope Dimitri had come up with something. He usually did. Leaving my thoughts about Mr. Vale at that, I tried to get back into the rhythm of the flashing lights of the television mast. But the magic of the evening was gone, so I finished my beer and went inside.

9

I arrived at the campus the next day at two thirty, half an hour before my appointment with Mr. Vale. I had decided not to bother Dimitri with the problem of how to deal with the upcoming visit. Surely I could solve this on my own. In any event stay friendly and polite, I instructed myself, and we would take it from there. To pass the time, I looked through my proof. Once again, it was a joy to read. As Dimitri said, it led directly into the high country of number theory; not only did it solve the mystery of the wild numbers, it provided research material for years to come. And if ever again I should be caught in an impasse, I had only to think back to this one discovery, which justified my choice to be a mathematician once and for all, not merely taking the sting out of past sufferings, but out of future ones as well. At a quarter to three, I sneaked one last loving look at my proof before storing it away definitively in the drawer of my desk. I did not want to provoke Mr. Vale unnecessarily.

I swung around in my chair to look out the window. On the field, a group of students were playing soccer. It was the hottest day so far this year, and their bare torsos glistened with sweat. The game was friendly and relaxed, and when the ball rolled out of bounds, it took quite some time before someone volunteered to retrieve it; meanwhile a bottle of Coke was pulled out from underneath a pile of clothing and was passed around in the thirsty group.

I looked at my watch. It was five minutes to three. In order to appear occupied when he arrived, I wheeled my chair over to the filing cabinet and extracted a stack of papers from the top drawer. They formed the record of my work of the past year, that is, of the uninspired period before the wild numbers had come into my life. I rode back to my desk and began to work my way through the pile. With great ceremony I crumpled up page after page and threw them in an elegant arc into the waste-paper basket. Among my notes on calibrator sets I stumbled upon Mr. Vale's solution of the Wild Number Problem. At the time, I had been so intimidated by his visit that I had stored his papers away without looking at them. Now I was amused by the crazy formulae, elucidated with deep statements such as "Wild numbers are the debris left by the collision between order and chaos," and "psyche equals energy times the Vale constant squared." It had become a document of historic value, for without it I would never have embarked on my journey into wild number territory. I opened the desk drawer and slipped it underneath my own proof. Should the coming conversation go well, I could pull out both proofs so that we could compare our fine work, as good friends.

Startled by footsteps in the corridor, I slammed the drawer shut and sat up straighter, all set to receive Mr. Vale. But the footsteps continued for a short distance past my door and I heard the jingling of keys: it was only Larry.

Looking out the window again, I spotted my prospective visitor approaching from the far end of the field. There was something unusually energetic about his manner. Of course, men in suits always look purposeful, and being rather late, he now and then quickened his steps, but there was something else as well, although I couldn't put my finger on it. He was headed straight towards the soccer game. Instead of altering his course, he walked through one of the goals, marked by two piles of clothing, and onto the playing field. The participants stopped to stare in amazement. Then as a joke one of them began to dribble the ball around the intruder as if he were an opponent. But the intruder ignored him, and with a fixed gaze walked out of the game through the other goal. The students pointed to their foreheads, shrugged their shoulders, and resumed play. When he had passed by my window and disappeared from view as he headed towards the main doors of the building, it finally occurred to me what made him so different today: for once he wasn't lugging around his enormous briefcase. Be nice to him, I instructed myself once again. Whatever names he might call you, stay polite.

Presently I heard his footsteps in the corridor. Without knocking he pushed open my door.

"Good afternoon, Mr. Vale," I said, rising to greet him.

Red in the face and out of breath, he approached the desk. Around the armpits of his jacket two large circles of perspiration had formed.

"Won't you sit down," I said. "Can I get you something to drink?"

With his foot he slid the chair that I had offered him aside. "Traitor," he said. The finality of his tone left little room for debate. This visit was not going to be easy.

"I'm sorry you feel that way," I began delicately, "now if you'll..."

Before I could say anything else, he had climbed onto the chair.

"Get down from there, please," I said, backing away.

"Traitor!" He jumped onto the desk, which creaked ominously under his weight. Burrowing his foot into the stack of papers, he sent them flying in every direction.

"Mr. Vale! Please!"

"Traitor!"

He dove onto me, his momentum pushing me down into my chair. We rolled backwards and came to a crashing halt against the windowsill. I was engulfed by the pungent smell of his sweat as he held me pinned against the seat. My feet searched helplessly for the floor, but every time I shifted my weight forward, the chair would roll backward, against the windowsill. The window above me bobbed and heaved like a porthole of a ship in a storm. With his jaws clamped tightly shut and a murderous look in his eyes, Mr. Vale closed his hands around my neck. The blood began to beat in my head, a red haze forming around my eyes. This was the end. No, it couldn't be, it mustn't be, not now that I had solved the Wild Number Problem. Mr. Vale tightened his grip, pressing his thumbs into my Adam's apple.

No. NO! I ground my elbow into his stomach. Choking and coughing he let go of me and staggered backwards towards the desk, swinging his arms in circles to keep his balance. I took in air with hungry gasps. My lungs were aching for more, but there was no time to lose. I had to get out of the narrow space between the desk and the windowsill. I grabbed hold of the office chair and barrelled it straight into him. But rage had given him superhuman strength, and with one mighty push he sent me flying backwards again. I stumbled and fell, dragging the chair down with me. Crawling over the carpet, I was lost in a maze of chair legs and table legs. Mr. Vale seemed to come at me from every direction, grabbing my ankles, clawing at my shirt, hooking his foot around my wrist to upset my balance. The door. I had to get to the door! When he lunged at me again, I turned abruptly and planted my hand full on his face, scrunching up his features with my fingers while trying to push him away. A quick jerk of his head made me lose my grip. Snarling like a dog, he set his teeth into my hand. I let out a piercing cry, my eyes flooding with tears as a sharp pain swept through me, growing more intense as his teeth sank deeper into my hand; I could feel the flesh giving way under the pressure of his powerful jaws, a curiously dead sensation at the core of the pain.

"What the hell is going on in here?" It was Larry. "Let go of him, you crazy son of a bitch!" In a blur of tears I saw a figure reaching down to grab my assailant by the collar. His nostrils flaring, his growls muffled by my hand in his mouth, Mr. Vale shook his head wildly this way and that, like a hyena trying to rip strips of meat from a carcass. Waves of pain splashed through me. Then suddenly all the pressure was gone and my arm dropped to the ground. Two struggling silhouettes moved along the window and disappeared from view.

I was lying on my side. The carpet felt rough against my lips, and a nearby paper clip made me go cross-eyed. Farther on lay the pencil I had lost some time ago, and beyond that I saw red, bright red. My fingers twitched. They were soaking in a warm, sticky pool that had formed on the carpet. With my other hand I reached for one of the table legs, cool round and smooth, coiling my body around it in an unsuccessful effort to pull myself up. I tightened my grip around the table leg, concentrating on the soothing coolness of the metal. Five plus three equalled eight. It always had and it always would. Seventeen minus thirty-one equalled negative fourteen. The set of wild numbers was infinite. If for a given set of pseudo-wild numbers...it followed that...if... I squeezed my eyes shut as a new wave of pain swept all thoughts away.

Beyond the pain, in another world it seemed, I now heard agitated voices, many voices, and screams, and at regular intervals great crashing sounds that left a metallic resonance, as if someone was throwing heavy burlap sacks into an empty truck. Letting go of the table leg, I rolled onto my back, stared up at the ceiling, and waited. Eight minus eight equalled zero. Zero times zero equalled zero. The screams were becoming throatier, squelchier, changed into gargles. And then the only sound was that of the burlap sacks.

"That's enough, Larry!" came Dimitri's voice loud and clear. "You're killing him!"

There was another crash, and another.

"I said: enough!"

There was a short silence, followed by a burst of distraught voices. "Call an ambulance! Call the police! Get some paper towels, quick!"

Hands were hooked under my armpits as I was hoisted into my chair. People were running in and out of my office, others stood and stared at me with their mouths hanging open. There were papers everywhere, all over the desk and on the floor, splattered with blood. Someone lifted my limp arm from the desktop and wrapped paper towels around it. In an instant red spots soaked through, spreading rapidly across the paper and merging. More towels were wrapped around my hand.

"Are you all right, Isaac?"

"Isaac?"

"Are you all right?"

It took an effort to find my voice. "I don't know."

Not everybody in the office was interested in me. Most of them were looking down at a heap of clothing flung against the filing cabinet. My gaze was drawn to the patch of striking colors at one end of the heap. With a jolt I realized it was a face, or rather what was left of it. One eye had been beaten closed and transformed into a bluish-white swelling, with pink around the edges. A steady stream of blood trickled out of one of the nostrils, collecting on the swollen upper lip before dripping onto the carpet. But the worst was the lower jaw, hanging at an odd angle from the battered face, with the row of teeth exposed–a glistening, nasty little row. The pain in my hand sharpened.

Sirens approached, louder and louder, stopping just beneath my window. Red flashes chased each other across the walls. "Stand clear! Everybody out!" People in white uniform and people in blue uniform entered. The heap of clothing by the filing cabinet was lifted onto a stretcher and carried out of the office.

I was helped out of my chair. Flanked by Dimitri and Harvey Mansfield, an artificial intelligence expert from the computer science faculty, I was led through a confusion of staring faces into the corridor.

"Easy now," Dimitri said. "You're doing just fine."

A woman with an enormous volume of curls and a mouth full of gleaming white teeth popped up out of nowhere. "Hi, I'm Anita Schreyer from the *Chronicle*. Could you describe to me what happened just now in your office?"

"Leave him alone," Harvey snapped at her. "Can't you see he needs a doctor?" He took a firmer hold of my good arm and we quickened our pace. The curt click of women's shoes accompanied us down the corridor. Did I know the assailant, she wanted to know, why had he attacked, had there been an exchange of words prior to the attack, how was I feeling.

She disappeared as suddenly as she had appeared. Doors opened and I was momentarily dazed by sunlight. Then I saw an ambulance driving off, and a group of young men standing in a semicircle in its wake, one of them holding a soccer ball in his arm. We crossed the field, the dry patches in the grass at times glowing like gold, then paling to a dull yellow, the surrounding green now and then darkening to almost black. I had become a giant hand, wrapped in an enormous ball of bloodstained paper towels. The rest of my body hung on like a useless appendage, my knees seemingly bending the wrong way whenever I took a step.

"You're doing fine, Isaac," said Dimitri, "We're almost there."

"Almost where?"

"The campus clinic," said Harvey.

"Is he dead?"

"Who? Oh, you mean that nut who attacked you? No, no, but he did take quite a beating."

We entered the clinic, where Harvey and Dimitri entrusted me to a nurse who led me through a door and sat me down in a chair. A rosy-cheeked young man in a white coat came in through a side-door. "Hello, I'm Doctor Greenwood," he said, pulling up a chair beside mine, "but I see we'd better not shake hands." Ever so carefully he peeled away the bloodied strips of paper towel. He whistled when he saw the wound. "How did you manage to do this?"

"I was bitten."

"By a dog?"

"No. By a human being."

"Good Lord."

Dr. Greenwood was one of those eager young doctors who had learned to explain everything as he went along: the name of the sedative he gave me, the reason for wearing rubber gloves, and so forth. What he said went in one ear and out the other, but his voice was a welcome distraction from the pain that I felt whenever he pressed an absorbent cloth against the wound. Once, when he removed a cloth that was saturated with blood, I caught a glimpse of a deep pink crescent-shaped gash running across the top of my hand. Immediately it filled up with blood again. When I looked away, I saw an after-image of the gash in complementary green, reminding me of the map of Death Valley in Dimitri's atlas. The Wild Number Problem. I had solved it. Thank God I was still alive to tell the story.

"It's just a flesh wound. The bleeding makes it look a whole lot worse than it really is," the doctor assured me, covering up the wound with a fresh cloth. "Human teeth are not very sharp: they cannot cut through tendon the way dog teeth can. You'll be able to use your hand just fine when it has healed."

The nurse meanwhile was cutting squares of gauze and dabbing them with some liquid from a brown bottle.

"Now for the bad news," Dr. Greenwood said with the cheerfulness typical of his profession. "The human bite may not be the sharpest, but it certainly ranks among the dirtiest. Our mouths are a breeding ground for all sorts of highly infectious bacteria. That means we cannot stitch the wound: those nasty little buggers would have quite a party in there. So what we're going to do is disinfect the wound as best we can and let it close by itself. Unfortunately this means it will take longer to heal and will probably leave quite an ugly scar."

He nodded to the nurse, who came to us with a tray full of medical instruments and fresh bandages.

"Now this may sting just a little," he said, picking up a square of gauze with tongs and placing it on my hand. As the disinfectant trickled into the wound, I flinched and drew in air through my teeth. For a moment everything went black.

The doctor waited patiently for me to return to my senses before going on with his explanation. "This whole area of your hand will feel very tender for a while," he said, "especially here." Keeping the gauze pressed against the wound with two fingers, he flipped my hand over to show me the arc of violently purple tooth marks in the ball of my thumb. It had not occurred to me, but Mr. Vale's bite had left injuries on both sides of my hand. The doctor removed a roll of bandage from its cellophane wrapping and wound its entire length around my hand, meanwhile giving me instructions. The most important thing was to keep the wound clean. Cleaner than clean. I was to have someone dress it for me regularly. If I ran a temperature or felt any swelling, I was to call a doctor immediately.

"Now I want you to sit still for a while," he said when he had fastened the end of the bandage with two clips. "You have just had a shocking experience. So relax and let the sedative do its work."

After the doctor had excused himself, the nurse offered me a mug of hot tea. Then she went about her business, humming to herself as she cleaned up the bloodied cloths and bandages and gathered the used medical instruments on a metal tray. Once I decided I did not have to converse with her, I relaxed and passed the time slurping tea while studying the posters on the walls advocating the use of condoms, recommending warm-up exercises before doing sports, warning against smoking. Thanks to the sedative and the reassuring antiseptic smell that came from the bandages, the pain in my hand was dulled to a faint throb.

Five minutes later the doctor returned to do some final tests. I was asked to follow his finger with my eyes and to tell him whether I felt any dizziness.

"No? Very good. Now I want you to stand up very slowly and to take a few steps. That's it. Easy does it."

He and the nurse stood by in case I needed support.

"Dizzy? Nauseated?"

I shook my head.

Dr. Greenwood handed me a plastic bag containing clean bandages and a bottle of painkillers, once again stressing the importance of keeping the wound clean and of warning a doctor at the slightest sign of infection, then wished me the best of luck.

Harvey Mansfield had disappeared, but Dimitri was waiting for me by the exit. The whole affair had shaken him badly: I had never seen him look so pale and worn. "I am terribly sorry about this," he said, as if it were all his fault. "How are you feeling?"

"I'm all right now."

"There's a police inspector in Larry's office who wants to ask you a few questions. Do you feel up to it?"

"I suppose so."

We crossed the field towards the Math and Computer Science Building. With my hand wrapped in an impressive bandage and with Dimitri by my side, the grass, the trees, the clouds and everything else around me seemed extraordinarily deep and pure. I remembered this way of perceiving the world from those rare occasions in childhood when I had hurt myself (sitting up in my room doing arithmetic, I ran little risk): once I was comforted and bandaged, the world looked wonderfully fresh and mysterious, as if for the first time I knew what it meant to be alive.

Sitting at Larry's desk was a policeman in a short-sleeved shirt busily writing on a notepad. He had hung his jacket over the chair and moved Larry's papers to the side to make room for his attaché case, taking command of the office space like a colonel who has declared a state of emergency.

Larry meanwhile was seated in the windowsill. With a frown he kept curling and straightening the fingers of his right hand. "Howdy, Isaac! That's quite a baseball glove you're wearing there. You okay?"

"I think so. How about you?"

"Oh, nothing too bad: the son of a bitch kicked me in the shin a couple of times and my knuckles are a bit sore. That's about all."

Dimitri and I had sat down opposite the policeman, who stopped writing and introduced himself as inspector Hutchinson. "Just a few questions, Mr. Swift," he said, leafing through his notes. "Let me see. Ah, yes. Mr. Oberdorfer was telling me just now that he saw the suspect in the hall yesterday in quite a rage, yelling, quote: 'Justice will prevail! Justice will prevail!' Do you have any idea what he was referring to?"

"I'm afraid I do." I told the inspector how three weeks ago Mr. Vale had come to my office with what he thought was the solution to an important mathematical problem (I considered the name of the problem irrelevant for a police report) but in fact was pure nonsense, and that yesterday morning he had accidentally caught sight of my genuine solution of the very same problem and accused me of plagiarism.

"Hey Isaac, what problem did you solve?" Larry butted in.

I had looked forward immensely to Larry chancing upon my discovery in *Number*. Now I had to break the news to him in person, under circumstances that could hardly be considered ideal. But he deserved to know: after all, he had saved my life.

"You solved the Wild Number Problem?" he exclaimed. "Are you serious?"

"Gentlemen, if you don't mind...," Inspector Hutchinson began.

"And you knew about this, Dimitri?" Larry persisted. "Shucks guys, how come you didn't let me in on it?"

"Gentlemen, could you please save this discussion for later? I have a very busy schedule."

"But this is outrageous, inspector! How would you feel if your colleagues didn't tell you they had finally cracked a famous old murder case?"

"I'm sure they would have their reasons."

"I give up," Larry sighed. "Go ahead with your inquiries."

"Thank you. Now if I understand your story correctly, the suspect claims that he was the one who solved this...uh...'Wild Number' problem and that you plagiarized his work."

"That is correct," I said.

"And?"

"And what?"

"Did you in fact plagiarize his work?"

"Of course he didn't!" Dimitri cried indignantly. "Isaac Swift is a first-rate mathematician. Mr. Vale is a seriously disturbed man."

"Please, Mr. Arkanov. Let Mr. Swift answer the question."

"No, I did not."

The inspector addressed his next question to Dimitri and Larry. "It is a well-documented phenomenon that plagiarists are often unaware of any wrongdoing. They are so thrilled by an other person's idea that they simply forget it is not their own. Do you think it possible that this was the case with your colleague Mr. Swift?"

"I wouldn't know, now, would I?" Larry said, turning his nose up at us.

"Impossible," said Dimitri. "The mathematical ideas that Mr. Vale presented to us every week were pure nonsense, totally worthless rubbish."

"Did you actually ever see Mr. Vale's solution of the Wild Number Problem, Mr. Arkanov?"

"No, but..."

"Then how can you be so sure that it was pure nonsense?" The inspector's triumphant smile looked very much like a mathematician's smirk, a similarity that was reinforced by the sniggering that came from the windowsill.

"I have both versions in my desk drawer," I told the inspector. "Would you like to see them? Then you can judge for yourself."

"Thank you, but I am not a mathematician."

"I assure you, you don't have to be a mathematician to see the difference between Mr. Vale's work and mine."

"Very well then."

"Hang on," Larry said, jumping down from the windowsill. "I'll get them."

"Something is bothering me, inspector," Dimitri said while we waited for him to return. "My dear colleague has just been violently attacked and seriously injured. He deserves our sympathy and full support. Why am I getting the unpleasant impression that you are asking him to prove it wasn't his own fault?"

"I am only doing my job, sir. As a mathematician you must appreciate my desire to gain absolute certainty in this matter. Suppose the suspect really did solve the problem and suppose there is a conspiracy against him, a number of faculty members protecting one another. Unlikely as it may seem, I must at least consider that possibility."

"Fair enough," Dimitri replied, "but that still does not justify violence."

"Of course not. What I am trying to ascertain is whether the suspect had reasonable grounds to believe Mr. Swift stole his theorem, in other words whether or not he can be held accountable for his actions. If so, he goes to jail; if not, he will receive mandatory psychiatric treatment. That is the only issue that we are trying to settle here. Whether or not your colleague is guilty of plagiarism is of no further concern to me."

"My apologies, inspector. I hadn't looked at it that way."

"Elementary, my dear Arkanov," said Larry, coming in just then. He handed the inspector two sets of papers, keeping a third set for himself as he returned to his perch on the windowsill. "I took the liberty," he said to me, waving with the fresh copy of my proof.

"I had a sneaking suspicion," I laughed. Sooner or later he would have laid eyes on it anyway, and besides, I was flattered by the sudden interest he was taking in my work.

"'Define pseudo-wildness as follows,' "he read aloud. "That's a crafty maneuver, Isaac. I like it."

Meanwhile the inspector glanced at my proof and put it aside. He spent considerably more time studying Mr. Vale's fabrications. As if their spirit had taken possession of him, he made the strangest faces. "This does appear to be the work of a madman," he concluded. "Still, I would like to hold on to both versions for a while."

"But why?" Dimitri demanded to know.

"I'd like to show them to a number of mathematicians who don't have direct ties with your university. Just to be on the safe side. We will of course return your work to you as soon as possible, Mr. Swift."

He stored all the papers in his attaché case, reached behind him for his jacket and got up to go. "Thank you for your time, gentlemen. And good luck with your hand, Mr. Swift."

When the inspector had left, Dimitri puffed up his cheeks and let them deflate slowly. "What a day, what a day."

"Make that 'what a year, what a year,'" Larry said without looking up from my manuscript. "Way back in September I warned you that Mr. Vale didn't belong here. As usual nobody listened to me."

"By all means rub it in, Larry," Dimitri said. "I deserve it. I should never have negotiated with him. He had no business here to begin with, and I should have sent him home when it was still possible."

"You can't take the blame," I said. "We all went along with the plan."

Larry cleared his throat, a needless reminder that he was the exception.

"Still it was my plan," Dimitri insisted. "I was far too keen on protecting him against psychiatric help when that was what he really needed. I let my own unpleasant experiences in that department cloud my judgement, and you, Isaac, were the one to suffer. And poor Mr. Vale too, for that matter. I can't forgive myself for that."

"But if I had concealed both copies of my proof in time yesterday, this would never have happened."

My words could not console him. Staring down at the floor, Dimitri withdrew into an impenetrable cloud of self-reproach.

It was hot and oppressive in the office. While Larry went on reading my manuscript, I closed my eyes, slowly dozing off on the throbbing rhythm coming from deep inside the bandages. But on the threshold between waking and dreaming Mr. Vale was waiting for me; I saw his bulging murderous eyes again, the veins on his forehead and his flaring nostrils, I once again felt his teeth sinking into my hand. A sharp pain pierced through the thick walls of sedation and I awoke with a jolt, my forehead cold with sweat.

Not wanting to ask Dimitri or Larry for help, I reached for the plastic bag and groped among the packets of bandages until I found the bottle of pills. I finally managed to flick off the cap with my thumb and to shake a few pills onto the desk, only just preventing them from rolling off the edge onto the floor. If taking a painkiller took this much effort, I wondered how I was ever going to manage changing the bandages singlehandedly. Then I remembered the barbecue at Stan and Anne's. There would be plenty of doctors to choose from. It did not matter that the painkillers would make me too groggy to socialize properly, or that the story of my injury would elicit amused commentary. I needed help with the bandages. More importantly, however, I was in desperate need of company. For I was scared, scared of being alone and seeing Mr. Vale loom up as soon as I closed my eyes.

The silence was broken by Larry's soft laughter. "Hey Isaac, are you sure you didn't steal this from Mr. Vale?"

"What?" Dimitri said, annoyed by being disturbed from his gloomy meditations. "Please, Larry, this is not the time for silly jokes."

"Oh, but I am dead serious," he said, his lips curling into a smirk. "I hate to rain on your parade, guys, but what I have been reading here is pure nonsense."

10

"It's right here on the first page," Larry said.

He had come down from the windowsill and taken a seat across from us. He spoke slowly and articulated his words with exaggerated care, as if Dimitri and I were below-average first-year students. "Here Isaac claims that all pseudo-wild sets are *K*-reducible. But to establish *K*-reducibility you need a fixed and independent point of reference, the so-called calibrator set."

"So I've heard," Dimitri said with mock seriousness. He had

been the one to introduce the concepts of *K*-reducibility and calibrator set to number theory.

Larry ignored him. With points to be scored, there was no time for other people's humor. "I suggest you both take another look at the calibrator set that Isaac employs in his proof."

"But why? Here Isaac constructs the set, here he shows that it is fixed and independent." Dimitri indicated the places on the page with two impatient sweeps of his hand. "Its further properties are irrelevant."

"Just take another look, okay?"

"Very well. If you insist." Massaging his forehead with his fingertips, which were trembling slightly, Dimitri brooded over the lines in question. I tried to do the same but kept losing track along the way, finding it difficult to concentrate. Inside the bandages, a sharp pain was cutting a path through the muffled softness of the sedative.

Just when I thought Dimitri was sinking into one of his deep mathematical trances, he started in his chair as if someone had pricked him with a pin. He picked up the first page of my proof and held it up at various distances from his face.

"Dimitri, you imbecile," he said to himself. "How could you have missed something like that?"

"Missed what?" I wanted to know. "What do you mean?"

He rose from his chair holding onto the desk with both hands, which were shaking badly now. "Show him Larry," he said, "I cannot stand any more of this." Without greeting us, he left the office.

Larry and I looked at each other in silence, as if to allow Dimitri time to walk the full length of the corridor and leave the building.

Then Larry clicked his tongue against the roof of his mouth. "Poor old Dimitri. This would never have happened to him five years ago."

His compassion was skin-deep. He was struggling to keep a straight face. This was the moment he had waited for: mighty Dimitri Arkanov having to acknowledge his, Larry's, superiority.

For a moment Larry seemed taken aback by my severe look, but he was quick to recover.

"So Isaac," he said breezily. "Have you spotted the error?"

"What error?"

Dimitri had turned my proof inside out. From every thinkable angle he had fired critical questions at even the tiniest details. Proudly the proof had stood its ground. Upset by Mr. Vale's violent outburst, even feeling responsible for it, Dimitri had let himself be intimidated by Larry's cocky tone. Maybe he even wanted to spot the so-called error, out of a desire for punishment. If only my hand weren't hurting so much–the effects of the sedative were wearing off fast now–I could have exposed the faultiness of Larry's arguments in an instant.

"There is no error," I now stated simply.

"Sure Isaac, there is no error," Larry said, holding up his arms in surrender. "Why don't you go on home, now. We'll discuss this some other time."

"No, Larry. I am not leaving this office until you show me exactly what you mean."

"Oh boy," he said, rolling his eyes. "A child can see it, but I guess we'll have to spell it out for you." Jabbing at my proof with the point of a pencil, Larry began to enumerate the properties of the calibrator set I had used. "And now we come to the fun part." He studied me closely for a reaction. "Your calibrator set, the set that you conjure up to prove there are an infinite number of wild numbers, must fulfill at least two requirements. One: it must contain an infinite number of elements, and two: all of these elements must be wild."

"That's ridiculous," I protested.

"It certainly is," Larry agreed cheerfully. "For it means that your proof is circular."

"No!"

"Can't get any rounder, my dear boy."

I was about to protest when the five or six lines of my proof that were at issue began to glow; with every throb of my wounded hand the ink seemed to blacken, while the surrounding text faded into a grey haze.

"You see it now, don't you?" Larry's voice was almost tender.

I kept staring at the lines wondering how I could have overlooked something so basic. Even more I wondered how Dimitri, the great Dimitri Ivanovich Arkanov of all people, could have missed it too. How could he have thought that this worthless nonsense led to the high country of number theory, to breathtaking panoramas? I winced upon recalling that glorious moment in his office, when he had reached for the bottle of cognac and turned to face me with tears in his eyes. You have done it, Isaac. You have actually done it.

Larry leaned over the desk to pat me on the shoulder. "Sorry pal. Better luck next time, I guess. Want a lift home?"

"No thanks." I rose from my chair, gathered the papers with my good hand, and stuffed them into the plastic bag with the bandages. "I am expected at a barbecue," I said as if making an important announcement, and walked out of Larry's office with as much dignity as I could muster.

"There you are!" A woman came running towards me from the end of the corridor. It was the reporter from the *Chronicle*, who had pestered us on our way to the clinic. "I've been looking all over for you."

"Leave me alone."

"Please, Mr. Swift," she panted. "Just a few words about the attack. Or would you settle for 'Mr. Swift refused to comment.' ?"

"Let him go," said Larry, who had emerged from his office. "Isaac has had his share of bad fortune for one day." Measuring the journalist with approval, his tone became milder. "But why don't you step into my office for a moment? Maybe I can help you."

The world looked the same as always from the back seat of the taxicab that was taking me to Stan and Anne's house. People went on waiting at bus stops, the buildings stood in place, the sun was still setting along the path allotted for it at this latitude and time of year. It made no difference to anyone or anything that an apparent new truth had just gone up in smoke. It didn't even make a difference to me. I was still in one piece, as if all thoughts and feelings were still happily in orbit, ignorant of the emptiness at the heart of the system, where a mere hour ago a brilliant theorem had shone. But the devastating shockwave was still to come, and was bound to bring back the darkness and confusion that I had hoped to have left behind forever.

The taxi turned onto the steep road leading into the richest neighborhood of town. Pompous mansions were alternated by sprawling bungalows, none of them even remotely affordable on a mathematician's salary. In my present state, I was not particularly looking forward to socializing with the rich and successful, but anything was better than going home.

I paid the driver and walked around the house to the back, where I stopped at the edge of the terraced garden to observe the party down below. Fashionably dressed women strolled over the flagstone pathways in twos or threes, sipping at their cocktails, ooh-ing and ah-ing at the flower beds around the romantic water lily pools, the work of a well-known landscaper Stan and Anne had hired when they bought the house in early spring. Most of the guests had already descended to the spacious lawn at the bottom of the garden, where they swarmed around a number of picnic tables laden with food and drink. Stan, wearing a chef's apron, was dumping a bag of charcoal briquets onto an oversized barbecue. The whole scene was bathed in the soft orange-pink light of a summer evening, making everybody look wonderfully smooth-complexioned and carefree.

I sniffed at my shirt: not too bad for an outdoor party, especially considering what it had been through today. Still I felt foolish, standing there with a plastic bag in one hand and with my other hand wrapped in bandages, the thumb sticking up as if I wanted to shake hands with everybody; I could have been a tramp who had cut himself on a tin can when reaching into a garbage can and was now coming to thank the kind doctors who had patched him up for free. Just as I was considering a stealthy departure – so far, nobody had taken note of me – Anne came out of the kitchen with a tray of snacks.

"My God, Isaac. What happened to you?"

She wanted to know everything. We strolled over the winding pathways, adapting our pace to that of my story, sometimes stopping to allow me to go into detail. The ladies who were admiring the flower beds craned their necks to catch what I was saying, and once in a while the more daring among them would come up to us and dally for as long as possible before snatching a fish-shaped cracker with caviar or crab salad from Anne's tray, but they were too discreet to stay and listen outright. By the time we reached the lawn at the bottom of the garden, many of the people had turned to look at me, the mysterious wounded guest who had taken up so much of the hostess's time.

"That's quite a story, Isaac," Anne said, loud enough for all to hear.

When Stan wiped his hands on his apron and came to greet me, others followed in his wake. Before I knew it I was recounting my adventure a second time, now to a whole group of people.

I suppose Mr. Vale's assault provided a welcome change from the usual cocktail chatter about careers, babies or plans to build extensions on homes. As my story progressed, more and more people crumbled off neighboring conversations to collect on the thickening circle of listeners around me. It was sad, but my injury earned me far more status and respect than I had ever had by talking about mathematics. Even Vernon Ludlow listened attentively, and his wife, who had treated me to nothing but withering looks at the previous party, now gazed at me full of awe and admiration, as did many other women. And there was no need to ask for help with the bandages. Stan and several other doctors had already volunteered.

I was at the part where Inspector Hutchinson was questioning me when Anne offered me a glass of fruit punch. After Stan had assured me that a little bit of alcohol wouldn't hurt, I eagerly put the glass to my parched lips. To drink fruit punch with one hand was not easy, however: I was unable to take the spoon out of the glass, so that it poked me in the cheek-bone, and when I tapped the glass with my fingers to dislodge the chunks of fruit that clung to the side, they tumbled against my lips all at once, causing the juice to spill over my chin and onto my shirt. Even my clumsiness was welcomed this evening: one woman pulled a handkerchief out of her purse, another held my glass for me while a third wiped my shirt clean.

I told my audience how Inspector Hutchinson had taken both versions of the Wild Number Theorem with him as evidence and then moved on to Larry's painful discovery of a mistake on the first page of my proof. This disaster on top of a disaster was intended as a climax, but the glint in my listeners' eyes now faded rapidly. I should have known. We were now back to mathematics, an abstract and dry anticlimax to a juicy story of insanity and violence. The overly familiar lack of enthusiasm left me cold, but it hurt me deeply when Stan returned to the barbecue without having offered me any condolences whatsoever for the death of my theorem. I expected more from a friend, especially from the friend who had come to my apartment in the middle of the night and encouraged me to take my findings seriously. Come to think of it, he was the one who had advised me to show my theorem to Dimitri rather than to Larry. An irrational anger rose within me, as if Stan were to blame for Dimitri's oversight and everything else that had taken place. Luckily, one of my listeners asked me about Mr. Vale's behavior earlier on in the year. I was forgiven the unexciting mathematical interlude and my resentment towards Stan evaporated.

My story triggered off all sorts of anecdotes about human bites. None of the doctors present had ever treated such an injury, but one of them had heard a story about a jealous toddler who had bitten his baby brother in the cheek, another remembered a case of an earlobe that had been bitten right off. When examples from real life ran out, people took recourse to fiction. One woman sketched a gruesome scene from a movie she had once seen in which someone's nose was bitten off. This reminded Vernon Ludlow of a hilarious horror comedy featuring a female cannibal who had an insatiable craving for young men's "You-know-whats."

In need of peace and quiet, I wandered off to get another drink. I was not alone for long: a new circle closed around me demanding an explanation for my injury. With every rendition of my story, the events of the afternoon became more abstract, as if I stood above what had happened instead of being the victim. I now made playful use of rhetorical devices: pausing in the right places, digressing to tease my audience, avoiding anticlimax by no longer mentioning the error in my proof.

Among this batch of listeners was an attractive brunette in a black dress who watched my theatrics with a conspiring smile, as if she knew I was hiding part of the truth. At first I did not recognize her, then I saw it was Betty Lane. She looked so much friendlier and prettier than at the previous party that her life must have taken some dramatic turn for the better. Maybe there was a new man in her life. But I was far too busy with my own story to inquire after hers.

After a while Stan came to tell me now was a good time to change the bandages; the coals were not yet hot enough to start on the steaks and he had nothing else to do.

He took me to the largest of their three bathrooms, where with a proud sweeping gesture he drew my attention to the salmon-pink marble tiles on the walls, forgetting that he had already shown me them on my last visit. Then he offered me a seat in front of Anne's make-up mirror.

"You're quite a star tonight," he chuckled, as he began unwinding the bandage. "You should get wounded more often."

Looking at my tired reflection in the mirror, I felt like a stand-up comedian during intermission. Now that I was far from the crowd and alone with a friend, the events of the day lost their comic value and regained their grimness. And the bottom line was still the bottom line. "I may be a star tonight," I said, "but that won't bring my theorem back to life."

"The damage is that bad, is it?"

I nodded glumly.

"So I guess you were right after all, that night when I came to see you. Right about being wrong."

"That's right. And Dimitri, the Russian mathematician you suggested I confide in, didn't even spot the error." Once again, anger surged within me, towards Stan and now towards Dimitri as well. Why hadn't he seen it? Why?

"We all make mistakes," Stan shrugged. "Sometimes a whole team of specialists will miss the most obvious diagnosis. Patients have died as a result."

His tone was light as ever. A dead patient? Too bad, better luck next time. Considering the subject closed, he threw away the dirty bandages and lifted my hand up, turning it towards the light. Then he peeled away the square of gauze, brown with dried blood. The unguent that Dr. Greenwood had applied to my hand had hardened into yellow crusts, and visible through the cracks was the raw pink of the gash. Gingerly, Stan pressed the surrounding skin in various places.

"Only a very slight swelling," he concluded. "I'm going to put a new bandage on now. You can easily leave it on till morning."

Having the wound washed and dressed anew was more of an ordeal than I had expected. After taking another painkiller, I followed Stan back to the party. My steps were uncertain and weak.

I pushed my way through the crowd to one of the tables, where Mrs. Ludlow ladled some more punch into a glass for me–this time without any chunks of fruit.

Nearby, a gay couple was whispering and nodding amusedly in the direction of my bandaged hand.

"We were just wondering how many times you have had to tell people what happened," the taller one confessed to me.

"Six, maybe seven."

"Would you consider making that eight?" said his friend. "Leon and I are dying of curiosity."

Obediently I began rattling off my story again. My throat was painfully dry, but when I took a sip of punch all I tasted was the alcohol. I was short of breath, and the ground under my feet seemed to be giving way.

Leon touched my arm for a moment. "You look pale. Shouldn't you be sitting down somewhere?"

"I'm all right, thanks!" I shouted, as if raising my voice helped me keep my balance. "...And so Mr. Vale climbs onto my desk, yelling 'traitor! traitor!'"

"Amazing!"

"And then he kicks a stack of papers – a year's worth of research results – all through the room..."

"Dreadful!"

"Out of the way!" Anne cried. The crowd parted to let her through. "Excuse me!" She was on her way to the barbecue with a platter stacked with thick slabs of steak.

When the raw meat sailed past at eye-level and I caught its faint, sweetish odor, the world began to spin. Faces melted into each other, laughing mouths linked to form a long chain of gleaming teeth, Betty Lane's bare shoulder became Leon's hand holding a glass, and then an anonymous shoe, and then everything went black.

"Isaac! I-saac!"

Something was preventing me from rolling over to get away from the harsh voice. Grumbling angrily, I opened my eyes to find Stan slapping me in the face. I was lying in the grass and he had knelt down beside me. We were surrounded by a ring of curious guests. It was difficult to discern their features against the evening sky and in the blue haze of barbecue smoke. With a hand in my neck Stan helped me sit up. He pressed a glass against my lips and let me take a few sips of water.

"You fainted," he said. "We're taking you inside so you can lie down for a while."

I shook my head. "I want to go home."

"I don't know if that's such a good idea. Why don't you spend the night here?"

"No." I waved his helping hand away and scrambled to my feet; when I staggered forward, the guests who were in my path edged back with uncertain smiles.

"I want to go home," I told them.

"Okay, fine," said Stan, laying his arm around my shoulders. "I'll drive you. Vernon, can you keep an eye on the meat till I'm back?"

"That won't be necessary," said Betty Lane. "I'll drive Isaac home."

The next thing I knew, I was sitting in her car. I was exhausted, and my hand was hurting again, but in spite of everything an old longing was stirred when she leaned over me to help me fasten my seatbelt. It was pleasant while it lasted, and for one mad moment I wondered whether the ride home was a ploy to seduce me.

"I appreciate this." My voice sounded muffled.

"I owed you."

We drove in silence past the homes of the rich, and descended towards the sea of lights where the ordinary mortals tried to make the best of life.

"You know, Isaac," Betty began all of a sudden, "passing out was probably the smartest thing you could do back there. Those people didn't give a damn how you were feeling, as long as you entertained them."

"Maybe not," I said, remembering their sudden coolness when I told them about the error in my proof.

"That's the way people are. They feed on the tasty parts of your misery and discard the rest, leaving you worse off than before. I wasted a lot of time figuring that out. I hope you don't make the same mistake."

"I'll keep that in mind," I promised vaguely.

"I don't know. Maybe you think I'm cynical. But I have found that pulling myself up by my own bootstraps works better than counting on sympathy and coming out disappointed every time."

We fell silent. Although my eyes were fixed on the road in front of us, I sensed that Betty kept glancing over at me.

"You know, Isaac," she began again, her tone now delicate, almost shy. "When I said that I owed you, I didn't just mean a ride home. I owe you an apology for my behavior at the last party."

"Never mind." The episode that was troubling her seemed eons ago.

"But I do mind. I was terribly ashamed of myself. The next day I almost asked Anne your phone number, but I didn't dare to. I was feeling shitty that night and shouldn't have come to the party in the first place, but I figured: if I go stand in a corner looking miserable, people will come and ask me what's the matter. They avoided me like the plague, of course, until Anne tried to play matchmaker and dumped us on each other. I was dying for a shoulder to cry on, but by that time I had given up hope. I hated everybody and everything, and took it out on you."

Betty's confession made other events of that fateful day come into clearer focus. While she went on to apologize for her dreadful behavior in my car, I put the scene in fast forward. I saw myself dropping her off at her parents' house and driving home depressed, watching TV and then entering my study for the first time in months. In slow motion I relived the fatal moment that I took the *Proceedings of the Third International Congress on Mathematics* from the book shelf to look up Heinrich Riedel's proof. That moment had marked the beginning of my fruitless struggle with the wild numbers. Or else it had been earlier that same day, when Mr. Vale had left my office after depositing his nonsense on me. That was when I had the flash of inspiration, that made me decide to apply Dimitri's new techniques to the problem. Now too, I was struck by a flash of insight, a flash of the destructive kind, wiping out a landscape instead of revealing one: I realized that the germ of my fatal error was already contained in that first moment of inspiration, for it was only thanks to my careless disregard for the properties of calibrator sets that any progress had been possible.

I wondered what would have happened if I had seen through Betty's bitchiness that night and offered her the shoulder that she longed for. Who knows, we might have ended up in bed together. Or if not, I would at least have driven home congratulating myself for my good deed and gone straight to bed, instead of embarking on my ill-fated exploration of the Wild Number Problem. All of this might never have happened. My reflections came to an abrupt halt when I realized that Betty had not said anything for a while, apparently expecting some sort of response.

"I'm sorry?"

"I asked you if you were all right."

"Yes, yes. I'm fine."

We were in familiar territory now. Betty was right: sometimes it was better to deal with pain on your own rather than in company. The pang of loneliness that I often felt upon entering my neighborhood offered me more solace tonight than all the guests at Stan and Anne's party put together. This was where I should have gone in the first place, this was where I belonged. Everything was mourning the death of my theorem: the rows of modest houses, silently watching the hearse go by, the neon street lanterns quivering with emotion, the trees, mad with grief, throwing their branches up towards the heavens.

"To the right," I said, "and right again just past that variety store."

There was a lump in my throat when my apartment building came into view at the end of the street. It was the saddest place of all, a sad and lonely building made up of sad and lonely units, "bachelor apartments," rows and rows of them, some lights on, some lights off, balcony beside balcony beside balcony, all of them identical, and yet my wandering gaze was drawn towards the one on the fifth floor, third from the right, and fastened on the dark square of my bedroom window.

Betty did not stop in front of the lobby but parked on the lot at the side of the building.

"I'm coming up with you," she explained. When she saw the surprised look on my face, she burst out laughing. "To make sure you make it up to your apartment in one piece. For all we know you might pass out again in the elevator."

When she had helped me out of the car, she put her arm around my waist to support me, and seemingly of its own accord my arm went around her waist as well. While my bandaged hand stuck out in front of us, as if to indicate the direction that we were to walk, my good hand could not quite come to rest on her hip, a light thrill interfering with its search for support. With my eyes half-closed, I let her lead me around the building; when we passed through a cloud of warm vapor coming out of the vent of the basement laundromat, I caught sight of Mr. Vale's body sprawled over the sidewalk just ahead. The ambulance people must have had second thoughts on their way to the hospital and ditched him, considering him my responsibility, not theirs. It was only when we came closer that I saw it was just an old raincoat.

In the elevator, I swayed on my feet trying to focus on Betty's face. Sometimes she had one eye, sometimes three. After helping me unlock the door to my apartment, she handed me the plastic bag with bandages.

Her face was now a soft blur. I bent forward to plant a kiss on her cheek. I aimed badly, pleasantly shocked upon feeling her moist lips against the corner of my mouth. Closing my eyes indulgently, I leaned against her with my full weight.

With a gentle but resolute shove of her fingertips she pushed me away. "Are you going to be all right, or will you be needing help getting ready for bed?" Her nurse-like tone left no room for misunderstandings.

"No thanks, I'll be fine."

"In that case, good night, Isaac. And good luck." After a quick kiss on my cheek, she turned and walked off to the elevators.

All of a sudden I was alone in my apartment. Afraid of becoming afraid, I switched on the lights everywhere I went and opened cupboard doors as if to make sure nobody was hiding there. Lights or no lights, the place was possessed: a smirking Larry was seated on every windowsill and ledge. Dimitri was a sad shadow that withdrew from whatever room I was just entering. There was no need to look around corners or inside cupboards to find Mr. Vale. He was much much closer than that. The pain in my hand bore the imprint of his teeth, and the rest of his body grew from there. The weight of my tired body changed into his oppressive weight, once again pinning me to the ground.

With great difficulty I undressed, hopping around my bedroom until I finally had my pants off. Leaving the ceiling lamp on, I climbed into bed. As I drifted off to sleep, the bed became a raft floating in a vast ocean. I felt the warmth of the sun shining red through my closed eyelids. But there was also a chill in the air, as if the sun were setting. An evil creature had emerged from the depths, had caught my hand in its jaws and was tugging at it, trying to pull me from the raft so that it could drag me down to the ocean floor.

11

Early the next morning, I was pulled out of a deep, dreamless sleep by the telephone. I got out of bed and hobbled to the living room to pick up the receiver. It was Larry.

"Have you seen it?" he asked excitedly.

"Seen what?"

"We're on the front page of the *Chronicle*!"

"I see."

Yesterday's events splashed into my drowsy consciousness like a wave of ice cold water, waking me up instantly.

"Just thought you might want to know."

"Sure. Thanks."

"I'll catch you later."

Without asking me how I was doing he had already hung up again.

I went to the bathroom to tend to my injury. Curiosity triumphed over fear, and I carefully unwound the bandages, holding my breath when the last part clung to the wound and I had to pull a little harder. Although the bite looked ugly enough, the pain had become more localized, and thus more manageable. By resting my wrist against the edge of the sink for support and with a fair amount of patience, I managed to wash and dress the wound. When I was done, I treated myself to a painkiller. Possibly I could have done without, but the day was going to be bad enough as it was.

After setting the table for breakfast and switching on the coffee machine, I went down to the corner store to buy a paper. "STUDENT BITES PROF," the headlines screamed, although the letters were of a modest size and darkness. The article itself was only two columns wide and did not reach the fold–it was just a juicy local anecdote, squeezed in between the latest national and international developments. I tucked the paper under my bad arm and reached into my pocket for the exact change that I had counted out at home, avoiding the shopkeeper's inquisitive look. My heart thumped in my throat all the way back to my apartment, but I postponed reading the article until I had sat down for breakfast, where I could wash the bad news down with coffee.

> A mathematics professor was assaulted in his office yesterday afternoon by a seriously disturbed student who suspected him of plagiarism.
>
> The problems began in September last year, when Leonard Vale, a fifty-three-year-old former high school math teacher, enrolled as a first year student at the university.

And so forth. It was all in there, his pompous manner of speech, the heavy briefcase and the tape-recorder, the weekly fifteen-minute sessions and Larry's refusal to take part in them, my work on the wild numbers –

> When Isaac Swift began research on the famous unsolved Wild

> Number Problem, he could not have envisioned how wild the outcome would be...

–along with an occasional comment from Larry on the whole affair:

> "There is an ethereal quality in mathematics that has always attracted disturbed minds," Mr. Oberdorfer explains, adding that if it had been up to him, Mr. Vale would have been barred from campus right from the start.

There followed a vivid description of the events that had taken place in my office. Anita Schreyer had done a good job. Her account made the pain in my hand sharpen as if I were being bitten afresh. As could be expected with Larry the main source of information, his coming to my rescue was described in spectacular and heroic terms. The nature of Mr. Vale's injuries was the first real news for me:

> Mr. Vale is currently being treated in hospital, having sustained a broken jaw, a severe concussion and possible brain damage from the confrontation with Mr. Oberdorfer. "I had no choice," so the young, athletic math prof defends his rigorous measures. "It was him or me."

With a shudder I recalled the ghastly sounds that I had heard as I lay bleeding underneath my desk, and Dimitri crying, "That's enough Larry, you're killing him!"

Mr. Vale's trial had not yet been scheduled, but in all likelihood he would be declared of unsound mind and sentenced to mandatory treatment in a psychiatric institution. The article closed with Larry's discovery of the error in my proof:

"The irony of it all is that Mr. Vale could have saved himself the trouble," Mr. Oberdorfer observes. "Swift's answer to the Wild Number Problem was as bogus as his own."

From beginning to end, Larry was the hero of the story, the only faculty member who had had a bad feeling about Mr. Vale all year, the muscleman who saved my life, the superior intellect who spotted the error in my proof. And it was only too true, as was his final remark that Mr. Vale could have saved himself the trouble.

I suppose I should have died of embarrassment. Instead, I calmly finished breakfast. Reading about my debacle had left me surprisingly unaffected.

This very state of calm made me apprehensive. As if I were looking out over a tranquil sea after an earthquake, resignedly waiting for the devastating tidal wave to come rolling in, I knew for certain that the consequences of yesterday's disaster would inevitably crash down on me. The only question was: when?

I had my second cup of coffee on the balcony–it was yet another fine summer's day–and looked across the park at the television mast in the distance. Red, white, red...I wondered how that bunch of flashing lights had ever inspired profound reflections. My fruitless attempts at serious thinking were disrupted by the telephone.

It was my mother. She had read about me in the paper and was terribly upset. "You poor thing," she kept saying. It was funny: those were the exact words with which she used to comfort my brother Andrew whenever he had hurt himself. After I had reassured her that my injury wasn't serious, she once again invited me for the Sunday dinner with Andrew, Liz and the children. This time she insisted that I come, and I gladly accepted, welcoming all forms of distraction.

Even before I was back on the balcony, the phone rang again.

"Hi, it's me."

Out of a million voices, I would always recognize Kate's. She too, had read about me in the *Chronicle* and wanted to know if I was okay. I chose my words with care, bracing myself for a withering psychological analysis of the incident, Mr. Vale providing the conclusive proof of her hypothesis that mathematicians were insane by definition. To my surprise, all she did was sympathize. Her only psychological remark was directed against Larry, whom she found "as puerile as always," the way he compensated his deep insecurity with arrogance and bravura. Though inwardly I enjoyed hearing this, I felt obliged to come to his defense. He really had saved my life, and everything he said in the article unfortunately was true. After a short silence she asked me how the rest of my life was coming along, meaning romantically. Betty Lane came to mind, although nothing much had happened last night. Kate laughed heartily at my cautious formulation that there were potentially positive developments in that department. As for her, she had been seeing someone now for half a year, a very sweet and sensitive astronomer ("I guess I have a soft spot for mathematical minds!"); their plans for the future were becoming "damned serious": marriage, kids, the whole works. When we were through discussing our love lives, Kate suggested that we get together some time. To talk about old times. Why didn't I call her some day when I was feeling better? It was one of those arrangements where both parties show a willingness to meet, there being a tacit understanding that nothing will ever come of it.

When I had hung up, I felt a pleasant kind of melancholy. Good old Kate. Not that I regretted that it was over between us, but there was no reason for bitterness either, especially now that her real voice turned out to have so little to do with the one that had lashed out at me while I was working on the Wild Number Problem.

The next to call was Peter Wong. I wondered what he could possibly want from me. First I had botched up a simple algebra problem on the board, and now the press had informed the general public about my shoddy work. Peter was eager to see my proof, much as I tried to persuade him that it had become absolutely worthless. Wild numbers had always fascinated him, and there was much to be learned even from unsuccessful attempts to crack the problem.

Five minutes later, Stan called to ask about my hand and to see if there was anything he could do.

Angela called.

My brother Andrew called.

All day, the phone kept ringing. It was heartwarming to receive so much attention, but the more people who called, the more I missed one who didn't. Every time the phone rang, I hoped it would be him. Normally when a faculty member was ill or in some kind of trouble, he was the first to call. Dimitri's silence made it all too clear how angry he was, or hurt, or both. His glorious reputation had been tarnished by my folly; we had become partners in error.

As I circled around the telephone wondering if I should call him instead, the doorbell rang. Hope flared briefly: of course! For something this serious he would come to see me in person! But through the intercom, I heard an unfamiliar name. A few minutes later, a bouquet of pink carnations was pushed into my arms by a pimply teenager wearing a flowered T-shirt with "Hermes Florists" written across his chest. After having waited in vain for a tip, he greeted me curtly and trudged off to the elevator. When I was inside again, I discovered a card fastened onto the wrapping paper with a pink ribbon, on which "Thank you" was written in curly pink letters. Thank you? Was this a practical joke or had there been a mix-up? Upon folding open the card, I let out a cry.

"Most esteemed Professor Swift," the note began. The only person who would address me in such a formal manner was Mr. Vale! In panic, my eyes skipped over the neatly handwritten text to the signature at the bottom: Clara Vale Richardson, Mr. Vale's sister. It was only then that I was capable of reading the whole note:

> Most esteemed Professor Swift,
> I am so very very sorry that it had to end like this. I am at a loss how to express the depth of my respect for you and your colleagues, who out of sheer kindheartedness sacrificed your precious time to make a poor lost soul feel a little less lost. Indeed, your faculty was like a second home to my brother Leonard. It is with great humility that I now ask you not to be too angry with him for what happened yesterday afternoon. He was too far gone to know what he was doing. If anyone is to blame for this tragedy, it is I, for he was in my care and I should have noticed much earlier that he was losing grip on reality. For what it's worth, please accept these flowers along with my humblest apologies for the pain that you have suffered. Wishing you a speedy recovery and all the best,
> Respectfully,
> Clara Vale Richardson

Her note brought tears to my eyes. If anything was going to make me break down, it would be an overdose of sympathy, not the mathematical catastrophe that had befallen me. I did not deserve all this attention, nor did poor Mrs. Richardson deserve to take the blame. Did she realize that my flirt with the wild numbers had triggered her brother's fit of madness? If he had not seen my Wild Number Theorem, he would not now be lying in a hospital awaiting his trial, doomed to be locked up in an institution, possibly for the rest of his life.

To appease my conscience, I reasoned that if it had not been the wild numbers, something else would have eventually led to his mental collapse. Although a perfectly plausible hypothesis, it did not relieve me of my sense of guilt. Moreover, Mr. Vale was not the only victim of my mistake.

I was arranging the carnations in a vase, feeling worse with every stem that I lowered into the water, when the doorbell rang again. "Hi, it's Betty," the intercom crackled. When I opened the door she was half-hidden behind a bag of groceries. She had happened to be in the neighborhood, or so she claimed laughingly, and thought I might be able to use some supplies. I invited her to stay for dinner. As I was not much use in the kitchen with only my left hand, she ended up cooking for me, waving away my apologies that I wasn't being a proper host. During the meal we were both nervous, our laughter louder and more frequent than necessary. It was hard to believe: instead of a lonely and painful day of soul-searching, I had been swamped with sympathy calls, had been thanked for my generosity with flowers, and now I was enjoying my first tête-à-tête with a woman in over a year.

After dinner we had coffee on the sofa, where I showed her the article in the *Chronicle*. Instead of dwelling on Mr. Vale's assault, as most people did, she asked me about the error in my theorem, assuring me that although she did not know much about mathematics, she knew more than enough about disappointments and rude awakenings to understand how I must be feeling. In her eagerness to prove this, she kept drawing parallels between my ill-fated theorem and her failed marriage. The way I had sacrificed everything to work on the Wild Number Problem reminded her of quitting her job to move to Paris with her husband. I had fooled myself into believing glorious times lay ahead; she had fooled herself into believing the European adventure would revitalize her relationship. I had overlooked the most obvious properties of the calibrator set on which my whole proof depended; she had overlooked the most obvious property of her husband, namely that he was an incredible jerk.

Just when she was running out of ways to match the fragments of our broken dreams and the conversation showed signs of wearing thin, there was another phone call. "My son," came a choked voice. For a moment I thought it was Dimitri at long last. It turned out really to be my father, calling from a holiday resort in the Yucatan. He had found a copy of the *Chronicle* in the hotel lobby and had been reading it just now by the swimming pool. To think that his very own son had been brutally attacked by a psychopath! His very own flesh and blood, who–it seemed like only yesterday–had sat on his knee asking him difficult questions about negative numbers and infinity. I could not help wondering whether this outburst of fatherly sentiment had been induced by a few too many margaritas. Still, it was nice to hear his voice, even when he lapsed into his standard confessions of guilt that I knew so well from his Christmas cards: it had been much too long since I had heard from him, and he knew he had not been an ideal father, but he loved me, and wasn't that what mattered most?

After I had hung up, Betty and I really had nothing left to say to each other. A charged silence in which we avoided looking at each other was finally resolved when she laid a shy hand on my knee.

She stayed the night. My injury did not allow for much in bed. In fact, all we did was cuddle up against each other. But it was wonderful. As I drifted off to sleep, weightless and mellow with love, the mathematical disaster that had struck so recently seemed light years away. And yet it was largely thanks to this disaster that I was now lying in bed with a woman, as if the force of the explosion had vaulted me into this sweet corner of the universe.

The next morning, in an overzealous attempt to bring back the atmosphere of the previous evening, I suggested we have champagne with breakfast. The bottle that I had meant to bring to Stan and Anne's party to celebrate the birth of my Wild Number Theorem was lying in the refrigerator.

"Don't tell me you believe in that romantic stuff," Betty laughed. Fearing she had hurt my feelings, she quickly added that it had been a wonderful night, but that she did not yet know what it meant to her, that given her previous experience she had become extremely careful, that we should take it a step at a time. I assured her that I totally agreed with her, and that the champagne had indeed been a silly idea.

After so much cautioning from both sides, our goodbye embrace was unexpectedly passionate.

Then I was alone, and silence reigned in my apartment. No more sympathy calls, no more flowers or women at the door. The period of grace was over; the time had come to face reality. Although I could not pluck up the courage to go down to my office and clean up the mess, I did walk to the fax service on the other side of the park to send a message to the editor-in-chief of *Number*:

> Dear Dr. Goldstein,
> You have just received or will shortly be receiving a manuscript from me, in which I believe to have proven a theorem.
>
> The proof unfortunately contains a fundamental error and is thus unsuitable for publication. You may consider my manuscript unsubmitted.
>
> Please accept my apologies for any inconvenience.
>
> Yours sincerely,
> Isaac Swift

Sending the fax had been quick enough to be relatively painless. I even had to laugh at the inconvenience for which I was apologizing, which would amount to throwing an unopened envelope into a wastepaper basket.

On my way home, I went for a walk in the park. By the water lily pond I sat down on a bench, hoping that the green surroundings would bring about a contemplative state of mind. The truckload of sympathy and especially Betty had cushioned my fall, but that did not relieve me of taking responsibility for what had happened. In tackling the Wild Number Problem, I had gone for broke; now I was broke. Somehow, I had to pay for my mistake. It was not honorable simply to await the day that the faculty board would recommend I start looking for another job. That day was bound to come, perhaps sooner than I thought.

Maybe I should say farewell to pure mathematics and move down the hall to Computer Science, to become an anonymous member of a team developing expert systems, or whatever it was that those guys did to make modern society run even smoother. Casting away my lofty ambitions, I would make myself useful for a change, a modest but vital cog in the machinery of progress. But would I be able to overcome my antipathy towards computers? Quitting university altogether was another option. I could always become a high school teacher (following in Mr. Vale's footsteps!), humbly passing on old truths instead of arrogantly striving to discover new ones. But I did not particularly relish the idea of standing in front of a classroom full of unruly teenagers, most of whom would drop mathematics if given the choice. Something more drastic perhaps, like going to a Third World country to teach arithmetic to orphans in a refugee camp? Either I lacked the courage to give up everything or the conviction that adding and subtracting would benefit those children, but the plan did not seem feasible.

I wasn't getting anywhere. If only I could speak to Dimitri. One single remark, one fatherly hand on my shoulder and I would know exactly what to do. It was painfully clear that he wanted to have nothing to do with me... unless he had been trying to reach me while I was sitting here in the park. That was wishful thinking. Once again, I considered taking the initiative and calling him. But what could I say? Should I apologize? What was embarrassing was that he was not entirely free of blame himself. Any confession from me would only confront him with his own unfortunate role in the affair.

Without having come to a satisfactory conclusion, I got up from the bench and left the park.

I bought flowers for my mother and tried to find presents for my nephew and niece. As Uncle Isaac had no idea what kind of toys were appropriate for a six-year-old and a four-year-old, he settled for chocolate. The family dinner took care of my Sunday evening. It was nice to see everybody again, and my worries about my future as a mathematician were momentarily drowned out by children's voices, happy and shrill.

Then, on Monday morning, there was no way around it, and I took a bus down to the campus.

Larry's door was open as usual, and I could see Dimitri was in too; the beam of sunlight that shone from his office into the corridor was broken by his moving shadow. Fearing that he was about to come out, I quickly unlocked the door of my own office and slipped inside. When my eyes had grown accustomed to the bright sunlight, I saw that the worst mess had already been taken care of by Dolores, the cleaning woman. Around the filing cabinet there was a patch of carpet that had become a paler blue from all the scrubbing, in which there were a few darker spots, presumably blood. Underneath my desk, where I had lain bleeding, there was another light patch, again with a few dark drops. All the papers had been gathered and left in an irregular stack on my desk, creased and torn and spattered with blood, Mr. Vale's and mine.

I resisted the temptation to throw everything out, a symbolic act that would have stamped the past year as entirely wasted. Instead, hoping for something that could be salvaged, I took the pages one by one and, using my bad hand as a paperweight, ironed out the worst creases with my other hand. Listlessly I began to sort them, with a vague plan to take up the thread of my modest earlier research on calibrator sets. Soon I lost heart, however, and with every new page that I picked up, my attention was drawn less by the mathematical notes and more towards the dramatic shapes of the bloodstains.

Like a series of Rorschach tests, they suggested all sorts of objects to me, and I tried to imagine how a psychiatrist would interpret them. Suddenly angry with myself, I swept all the pages back into a single pile. There was only one psychological explanation for what I was doing: I was staring at these bloodstains to postpone the painful but inevitable confrontation with Dimitri.

Larry did not notice me passing his office. His mouth wide open, he was about to set his teeth into an enormous submarine sandwich. Grateful that for once I was spared his wisecracks, I continued down the hall to Dimitri's office.

I stopped in the doorway and stared in disbelief at the scene inside. There were books and binders stuffed with papers everywhere: on the desk, on all the chairs, and crammed onto the windowsills. Dimitri was walking back and forth between the partially dismantled bookcase and the growing towers of cardboard boxes. It seemed as if he had aged over the weekend, as if he had lost weight and his hair had grown thinner.

"Oh, is that you, Isaac," he said, finally taking note of me. "How is your hand?"

"It's fine," I said. "But what are you doing?"

"I am doing what I should have done several years ago," he said with a tired smile. "I am retiring."

"Because of... my proof?"

He got down on his knees to fold a new cardboard box into shape, then reinforced the bottom with a strip of adhesive tape. "The art is to quit while you're ahead," he said. "Years ago, I made myself a solemn promise that I would quit before making silly mistakes."

"I should be the one to hand in my resignation," I protested. "You shouldn't be paying for my mistake."

"I'm not. I am paying for my mistake."

His reassurance did not soften my anguish. Losing Dimitri was the worst conceivable punishment for my mistake, far worse than moving down the hall to Computer Science or leaving university altogether.

"Don't you see, Isaac? This wild number business was a first sign. To have missed such an elementary error is unforgivable. And it's only going to get worse. I cannot bear to stand by and watch my mathematical powers slowly fade away. No, it is better to turn my attention to other matters while I can still do so of my own free will."

As if to emphasize his resolve, he fetched a new load of books and bent over to lower them carefully into the freshly folded box. When he saw the troubled look on my face, he nodded amiably. "No hard feelings," he assured me. "None at all. I have spent many happy years in the realm of numbers, now the time has come to leave. Mathematics has brought me everything I hoped for and much much more... except the solution to the Wild Number Problem, of course. I thought I had learned my lesson thirty years ago, when the wild numbers warned me that my mathematical powers had reached their limit, warned me that mystery should not be attacked head-on but approached in a roundabout fashion and with humility. I suppose I needed a reminder." Looking around the room, he scratched himself behind his ear. "Dear me. I have been packing all morning and the mess is only getting worse."

As Dimitri studied the titles of the last books remaining on the top shelf, a voice within me cried: What about me? What am I to do? I stopped myself from speaking out, however, not wanting to sound like a child forever begging for candy, regardless of the gravity of the occasion. As a witness to a dramatic moment in another man's life, I had no right to shift the spotlight onto myself. Instead, I remained in the doorway and watched how he went on packing his books.

"I don't suppose there is any point in asking you to reconsider," I said.

"Out of the question."

I tried desperately to find words to express all that Dimitri had meant to me over the years, to tell him how terrible I felt that it had to end this way, to capture my deep respect and love for him in one succinct phrase.

"The faculty won't be the same without you," I stammered.

Dimitri had not even heard me. He was down on his knees again, peering into one of the boxes with a puzzled expression. "What are these books doing in here? These were for the library, this one I was taking home. Unless you want it." He held up a thick algebra textbook from the nineteen-fifties. "No, I suppose not," he said, throwing it back into the box. "And what on earth is this? Goodness, now I have to unpack these as well."

When I left his office, he was crawling over the floor, trying to find the right box for the books clamped in his hand.

12

It is September. My first-year class started this morning. As the new students timidly entered the classroom–there were only three girls this year–I kept an eye on one particular seat in the front row to see if an older man with a heavy briefcase would sit down there. But the chair remained empty.

After class I had a meeting with Harvey Mansfield, the artificial intelligence expert who together with Dimitri had accompanied me to the campus clinic to have my hand injury treated. A couple of weeks ago I ran into him on the front steps of our faculty. We had never had anything to say to each other before, but on this occasion he asked me how I was doing and we ended up talking about our research. He was especially interested in calibrator sets, which he believed might contribute to refining a certain group of computer languages. One thing led to another, and we are presently working together on an article, which will hopefully appear soon in the *New Journal of Artificial Intelligence*. It isn't exactly *Number*, and I still have my reservations about the field, but at least my work is moving along again.

This afternoon I was in my office going over my contribution to the article when Peter and Sebastian dropped by. During the summer holidays they had devised a method with which they hoped to tackle the Wild Number Problem. For a moment I was dumbstruck. That they had come to me, of all people. But there was something disarming about their shamelessness, and I couldn't really be angry with them. When they eagerly began unfolding their idea, however, I had to stop them right away. It would never work, but to see why required a thorough understanding of Riedel's theorem on tame numbers.

They looked at each other, both hoping the other would speak up first. It was Sebastian who finally asked me if I would be so kind as to explain it to them.

I hesitated. Since the unfortunate events earlier this summer, I had banished the wild numbers from my mind. Besides, I was planning to go into town to look for a present for Stan and Anne. Time is running out, the wedding is only a week away.

So as not to disappoint Peter and Sebastian, I consented nevertheless, assuming that I would soon be finished: they were bound to lose the thread of Riedel's argument after a few steps. To my astonishment that moment did not occur. Two hours and forty-five minutes later, we had run through the entire proof. Peter and Sebastian had no further questions and left my room in high spirits.

It was late. I was too tired to go shopping for Stan and Anne, so I went straight home. The sun had already set when I made my way to the park for my daily jog. Sometimes my mind clears when I run, sometimes an annoying thought will haunt me all the way. Today, I thought about everything and nothing.

After having showered I settled with a beer on my balcony. It was a mild evening for the time of year.

Tomorrow night Betty and I are going into town to celebrate my birthday.

Thirty-five plus one equals thirty-six.